The Sacred Disc

The SACRED DISC

Charles West

SALVO PRESS
Bend, Oregon

THE SACRED DISC

Salvo Press
P.O. Box 9095
Bend, OR 97708
www.salvopress.com

Library of Congress Catalog Card Number: 99-68297

ISBN: 0-9664520-4-6

Printed in Canada
First Edition

To Denise, Gina, and Kristen

Chapter 1

They looked at the diplomas and certificates behind me when they came in. My brother, the doctor, fills up his office and every available wall in his examining rooms with diplomas and certificates. He says it reassures the patients as to your competence and abilities. That's all very well and good for a doctor, but how much assurance are a bachelor's degree in Physical Education, a master's and a Ph.D. in History and an honorary Doctorate of Divinity for a private investigator?

I was a little nervous. These were only my second clients as a private investigator, and the first to actually come to my office. Although the Anderson Agency: Collections and Investigations was established in 1960, I had only been with the company for the last three years, and then only in the Collections Division. I was the head of the Collections Division, a division which was comprised of one employee beside myself. Mr. Anderson was the entire Investigation Division, although I was never really sure what he had ever actually investigated.

"Holly, hold all my calls, please," I called out. Holly was the collections staff. It was the first time I'd ever given such a command and I think it caught her by surprise, as she came into my office and unplugged the phone on my desk.

"I'm leaving," she said. "I have to pick up Chris." Her son. "I'll lock the front door." There were no goodbyes as she walked out of my office. Moments later, we could hear the metallic chink of the front door being locked.

Now I could get down to business, whatever it was. Before me sat three men who looked as though they did not belong in the same room together, here or anywhere else. On the right was the Yogi Ben Barr, co-founder of the Eternal Truth Temple. The Yogi was dressed in a floor length white robe and wore a white muslin turban over jet black hair. The Yogi needed a shave.

On the left was the Baba Der Ursus, the other co-founder of the Eternal Truth Temple. The Baba was a distinct contrast to the Yogi. The Baba was attired in black. Cotton pants topped by a long black coat with sort of a Nehru collar. His close cropped blond hair was uncombed. I didn't know they made black Birkenstocks.

I hadn't been a detective for very long, but I had a hunch these guys weren't really from India.

The character in the middle was Cooper Page, attorney-at-law. Apparently the good fashion sense of his clients had not rubbed off on Page. He had on yellow pants, white shoes, a green plaid jacket and a tie with red stripes.

Like many lawyers, Page had a specialty. His could be described as "religious law." He specialized in either suing or representing members of the clergy, churches and now, apparently, more marginal elements of the religious community such as the Eternal Truth Temple. Page wanted to represent me once in a church related legal matter but I chose a lawyer who looked more like a lawyer than a used car salesman.

"Bob, I'm glad you could meet with us on such short notice," Page said.

Like I had so much else to do.

"No problem," I said truthfully.

"As you probably know," Page said, "this is the Yogi Ben Barr."

The Yogi bowed his head. "You may call me Yogi," he said.

"And this is the Baba Der Ursus, of course."

Of course.

The Baba clasped his hands together and bowed. "Call me Baba."

Yogi and Baba.

"If you don't mind," Page said, "I'm going to give the Yogi and Baba a brief summary of your life and experiences so that they may better gauge your karma as the proper person for this situation."

"Well, I haven't exactly said I'd take the case yet," I said, worried about the acceptability of my karma.

"Of course we're willing to compensate you for your time here this afternoon. Shall we say..." He paused looking for a figure without wanting to commit himself to a number.

"Oh, whatever your hourly rate is would be fine," I suggested, knowing it was considerable.

Page swallowed and blinked. "Of course, that would be acceptable."

Of course.

Yogi and Baba did not react. Either they didn't know Page was charging them, or didn't care.

"Your father was a career soldier and you grew up on army bases around the country and the world. In high school you were an outstanding athlete. You then attended Kaweah Community College where you were on the basketball team."

Page was speaking as though he was speaking to me, but this information was meant not for me but for the two holy men on each side of him.

"After leaving Kaweah, you entered the Army and served in Vietnam where you were decorated and wounded. After your combat duty you served as a chaplain's assistant.

"Following your discharge from the service you enrolled at Sierra Pacific College, a church-affiliated institution in the foothills near here, where you were on the basketball team and received a degree in Physical Education.

"You then entered graduate school at San Joaquin State University and earned a master's degree in History. You then went to work for Kings Canyon University in the history department. During your time there, you earned a Ph.D. in History from the University of California at Berkeley, published a book about

Vietnam, you were married, and went to work for the Ben Carrick Ministries. Later, Kings Canyon University became Ben Carrick University. Then you had a falling out with Carrick. In fact, you were accused of trying to kill him, but such charges were dismissed. You then wrote another book, an exposè on the Ben Carrick Ministries, and appeared on several television programs in regard to those revelations. Last year, or so, you became a partner in the firm of Anderson Investigations and Collections. Upon the recent death of Mr. Anderson, you became the owner of the company. And that brings us up to the present. Is that pretty much it, Bob?"

"More or less," I said. Then remembering I was on the time clock at Page's hourly rate, I decided more might be better. "Well, actually," I said, "I went to Sierra Pacific College because it was the only school to offer me a scholarship. When you say I 'entered' the army, we used to call it getting 'drafted.' After Vietnam I was a clerk and chaplain's assistant. Then your chronology gets a little fouled up. After I got my master's from San Joaquin State, I went to work at Kings Canyon University as a lecturer in History, teaching History I for freshmen and a course on Vietnam and working as an assistant athletic director, trying to recruit tall Christian boys to play basketball for good old KCU, may it rest in peace.

"The chaplain I worked for in the service had become a dean there and helped me get the job. While I was there I entered the doctoral program at Berkeley. My dissertation was about Vietnam. It was later published in a slightly different form, by the

Kings Canyon University Press. Then Ben Carrick came along, endowed the university with a lot of money for a Telecommunications Department, with himself as a professor.

"Soon after, Kings Canyon University, which had been struggling financially for years, became Ben Carrick University, after another larger infusion of cash. Carrick, incidentally, personally awarded me with the honorary Doctor of Divinity Degree that no doubt caught your eye on the wall over there." I pointed. They looked.

"My ex-wife, Patty, was a member of the entourage Carrick brought with him. We married. Carrick began a foundation for Vietnam Veterans and appealed for money on his television ministry, on which I was an occasional guest. It helped my book sales. I thought it was helping veterans. However, I discovered that most of the money collected for the veteran's thing was being directed to Carrick's ministry, and therefore, to Carrick himself. I chose to confront Carrick with this on his television show. As I did so, his bodyguards tried to remove me from the set. In the scuffle I grabbed Carrick, hit him a couple of times and put his eye out."

"Put his eye out?" The Baba spoke.

"Yes, accidentally. As I was holding him, the bodyguards tried to pull me away and we all fell down and my thumb got jabbed into his eye and he lost the sight from it."

"That's why he wears an eye patch," Page told them.

"Kind of odd to me," I said, "that no one ever questions a faith healer with an eye patch."

"Anyway," I continued, "it was all captured on videotape. I was charged with attempted murder, but I was not convicted."

"Why not?" The Baba again.

"My defense presented the facts I had uncovered on Carrick's finances, and the fact that if I had wanted to kill Carrick, I certainly could have done a better job of it. It was something I had been trained for, after all, and a thumb in the eye wasn't one of the most effective methods taught. Carrick never had to do any jail time, either," I went on. "He had to pay some fines and was suspended by his church for a year, but he's back in business now. My wife divorced me, stayed on with Carrick ministries. She claimed she helped me with the book, and got all past and future royalties from it. It is still in print by Carrick Publishing, although my name no longer appears on the title page.

"I wrote a book about Carrick's veteran scam, which went through two quick printings before the publisher went on to the next scandal. I appeared on *Nightline* and the *Today Show*. Made some speeches around the country. By the time Carrick's church suspension was up, I was out of work. No college or university wanted me. I thought about teaching high school but I figured I had enough danger in Vietnam. So then Frank Anderson, whose son I had recruited for KCU, offered me a job at his collection agency.

"All I had to do was to call individuals or businesses and convince them to pay their delinquent debts. It worked well when they learned I was the guy who tried to kill a preacher on TV because of money. When Anderson died last year, he left the business to me. His son left KCU when it became Ben Carrick University, and went to Santa Cruz where he owns a futon store and is the tallest surfer on the beach. Anderson left him some other properties, so he did all right. He didn't want any part of the collection agency. So, I've got it now. And frankly, if I do take this case, I should tell you, this would be only my second case as an investigator."

"How did the first one come out?" the Baba asked.

"It was a church embezzlement," I said. "The assistant pastor made off with some church funds. I found him and brought him back."

"And the money?" The Baba again. The Yogi seemed to have no curiosity at all.

"He spent some of it. I traced him to Laughlin, Nevada, where a quick check of the dozen or so hotels made him easy to find, especially since he was using his own name. He wasn't violent or anything. He was a Seventh Day Adventist. When I found him he was eating meat, watching movies, drinking beers, and gambling, all against the tenets of his faith. And all on Saturday, his Sabbath. I took him home without incident and the newspapers or courts were never involved."

"That's what we are looking for in this situation," Page informed me. "Discretion. We certainly don't want to further tax the already overburdened legal system or be splashed across tasteless tabloid headlines. Yes, discretion is what we are looking for. And since you have accepted a fee for our conversation, the rules governing client privilege apply, and you are, therefore, bound not to divulge anything said here this afternoon."

No wonder Page had been so quick to offer a fee. And I snapped it up like a starving carp.

"No problem," I said.

Chapter 2

"It seems," Page said, "that the original text of the Temple's beliefs is missing."

"It is the sacred text of our faith," the Baba said, perhaps believing that Page wasn't fully communicating the importance of the missing sacred text. "It is the foundation of our belief, faith and way of living. It is irreplaceable and priceless. Perhaps you have read it?" the Baba asked me.

"No," I admitted. "I'm afraid not." I failed to mention that I often had the opportunity to purchase a copy from the Temple's smiling pilgrims at airports.

"So we are prepared to do whatever it might take to get it back, including paying a ransom, within reasonable limits, of course," Page said.

"Of course," I agreed.

So much for priceless.

"We are prepared to retain your services for a minimum of two weeks at this figure." Page wrote a generous figure on one of those yellow writing pads associated with the legal profession. "At the end of those two weeks we will evaluate your progress and make a decision then as to whether to continue or terminate the relationship. If you find this arrangement agreeable, I have a contract which you may review and sign later. We must remind you that time is of the essence in this situation, of course."

"That sounds fine to me," I said, "but I'm going to need a little more information about the text and any thoughts you might have about who might have done this."

"Of course," Page said. "The text is on a computer disc."

"A computer disc," I said in slight astonishment.

"A five and a quarter inch double-density, double-sided computer disc," Page continued, "commonly referred to as a 'floppy disc.'"

"A computer disc?"

The Baba interjected. "We used the available technology of the times, just as stone tablets or the Dead Sea scrolls were the available media of their time."

"Of course," Page commented.

"Since a single floppy disc will be difficult to locate," I said, "perhaps you have some idea as to who might be responsible."

"We pretty much know who is responsible," the Baba spoke up, a new edge to his voice. "It is a small group of former 'pilgrims' who are pursuing their own evil agenda with a vicious slanderous campaign of libel and criminal activities."

Page took over. "There is a small group of former Temple

members who have disrupted legitimate church activities, such as attacks on pilgrims involved in church business, vandalism and destruction of church property. They are called the Temple Justice Committee."

"We believe," the Baba said, "that the Committee is being funded by the government as part of their continuing campaign of surveillance and harassment to destroy our church and stifle religious freedom in our country."

I thought the Baba was going to deliver a speech, but he was interrupted by Page who handed me a computer printout and four file folders. "This is a list of known committee members and some basic information about each of them." The basic information included addresses, present and past, relatives, social security numbers, telephone numbers and a brief narrative on each of them, labeled "Psychological Profile." Talk about surveillance and harassment.

Chapter 3

The list of committee members was not long, and only four of them lived in the city. This made my job easier, I thought. I called the first name on the list, Christy Baker. The list was alphabetized.

I told her I was an investigator looking into the Church and that I needed to speak with her to get some basic information on the Temple and the work of the Committee. I neglected to tell her I was working for the Temple.

I arranged to meet her at the Cafe Midi, a coffee shop which was about halfway between where she lived and my office. The Cafe Midi was in what was called the Tower District, an older commercial and residential area so named because of the Tower Theater, a vintage art deco movie theater whose neon lit tower stood at the center of what served as San Joaquin's Greenwich Village or North Beach. Bookstores, specialty boutiques, antique stores, art galleries, restaurants, brew pubs, coffee shops and two small repertory theaters inhabited the spaces formerly occupied by those retail merchants now found in malls. Other similar neighborhoods had fared less well, populated by thrift shops, storefront churches and boarded windows.

I got there first and took a sidewalk table. The Cafe Midi was an old fashioned coffee shop, recently purchased by a gay yuppie couple. They retained the fifties charm of the old place, but changed the menu, reduced the cholesterol and raised the prices. It was now patronized by college students, would be poets, aging hippies and yuppies who wouldn't live in this neighborhood but came for the theater, clubs, galleries and the quest for the perfect cappuccino.

I saw her walking up the sidewalk. I didn't know if that meant she didn't have a car or if she parked around the corner. I knew it was her because her file included a photograph. She had short brown hair. It was curly and soft looking with a kind of unkempt quality to it that probably took a lot of care and preparation to maintain. She was wearing a red pullover top with tiny black polka dots. She wore Birkenstock sandals with no socks. Her pants were thin white cotton and in the bright San Joaquin sunlight you could not only see the outline of her panties, you could practically count the petals on the floral design. She was no kid, twenty-two. She must have realized when she got dressed, even when she purchased the pants, how transparent they were. "Why do women do the things they do?" I wondered. I'm sure I would come back to that question some time in the future; it had certainly come up enough in the past. I now needed to concentrate on the less cosmic mystery—the missing sacred text computer disc.

"Ms. Baker?" I made it into a question.

"Yes?"

"I am Bob Fisher. I called you."

"Yes. How did you know it was me?" she asked.

"I guessed," I lied. Who knows. Maybe I have a future in the investigation business.

I ordered a coffee for her, and a Diet Pepsi for myself. I hate coffee.

"What would you like to know?" she asked me.

"I just need a little information about your committee, what its origins are, what is its purpose. What its intentions are. That kind of thing."

"Who do you work for?"

"I am a private investigator, and I'm not really at liberty to name my employer at this time."

"Do you work for the Temple? Are you investigating the committee for the Temple?" she asked, her voice rising.

"From what I understand, the Temple probably knows everything possible about the committee already without my help," I said.

"That's true," she said, her voice returning to its normal level.

Maybe I did have a future in the investigation business. Again, I didn't tell the truth without actually lying.

"Is the committee involved in disrupting any of the Temple's activities?" I asked.

"Like what?"

"You know, demonstrations, rallies, that kind of thing."

"No, not really. We just don't have the numbers to stage an effective street demonstration. Ours is mostly an informational service, through the media."

"What about disruptions?"

"What do you mean?"

"Like the anti-abortion groups. Blocking entrances, or harassing members in their activities."

"No."

"How about more subtle tactics like break ins, messing with their computer system?"

"I'm not sure what you're getting at, Mr. Fisher."

"I'll tell you what he's getting at," a young man in his early twenties interrupted. "He's working for them, Christy."

"Who is he?" I asked her.

"This is Tom Hammerhill. He works for the committee, too."

"He knows that. He must know all about us," Hammerhill said.

It was partly true. I knew much about the both of them from the extensive, if somewhat biased, files provided by the Temple. I didn't recognize Hammerhill right away because his appearance had changed since they took the photo they had of him. His hair was longer now, much longer, and he had a beard. Temple members sported a more clean cut image, which I am sure was designed to help raise donations.

"He's one of them," Hammerhill accused.

"I'm not one of anybody," I said defensively. "I'm looking for the Sacred Text of the Temple. Perhaps you remember the Sacred Text?"

"What makes you think we have it?" she said. I assume that 'we' meant the committee.

"I never said you had it. That's the way an investigation works. I ask questions to people who may know something, add all the answers together and then I might find what I'm looking for."

"Well, she doesn't know anything. We don't know anything. Come on, let's go." He grabbed her arm and pulled her up.

"Let go of my arm."

Now I stood. "Let go of her arm," I said, and grabbed his arm.

"Let go of me," he yelled. He released Christy, so I released him, but then he started sticking his index finger in my face and yelling at me. "Listen, old man, you can't come around here intimidating anyone! We don't answer to the fucking Temple anymore! This is my girl and we're leaving and if you ever come near her or me again, I'll kick your ass up between your shoulder blades!" Still waving his finger in my face, he grabbed Christy again.

"Let go of me, goddamit!" she protested. "Who the hell do you think you are?"

Hammerhill had crossed my patience threshold, and he called me an "old man," so I grabbed his waving index finger and bent it backwards farther than it was normally designed to go. This resulted in Hammerhill simultaneously releasing Christy and sitting down in Christy's seat.

"If you get up or touch her again, I'll break all your fingers."

"He'll do it, Tom. This is the guy who tried to kill that TV preacher."

This was one of the benefits of having the reputation of a violent maniac. Your reputation precedes you, and is generally believed. Tommy Hammerhill seemed to believe it as he did not get up.

I handed Christy one of my cards. "I don't really give a shit about the Temple or what it does. I'm just looking for the Sacred Text. It is on a computer disc. If you think of anything, or just want to talk, give me a call."

I put ten dollars on the table for a cup of untouched coffee and tip for a nervous waiter. I picked up the Diet Pepsi and downed it in a single gulp, and walked away. I had left my car in the Tower Theater parking lot where it had collected a flyer for an upcoming reggae concert and an invitation to join the Jehovah's Witnesses. I threw them in the back with more just like them.

Chapter 4

I drove my car back to the office. It wasn't a long drive and I could have walked it. If I were in New York or San Francisco, I probably would have walked. I made a decision right there to walk more often. It would be good for me and good for the environment. Then the radio said that the temperature would be 104 today and tomorrow, a typical May springtime day in the city and valley called San Joaquin.

The office was a nice, two-story building. When it was built in the early sixties, the area was a prime office, and residential area. But as the city sprawled northward, most of the prestigious tenants moved with it. When Anderson left me the business it included the building. The only tenants now, however, were the Anderson agency, a telephone answering service, and an office of the American Lupus Foundation, a charity. That left three vacant offices on the ground floor that I periodically rented to political campaigns, which seemed to come along with alarming frequency, and an occasional community service organization, depending on funding, or some fly-by-night building contractor or something.

I lived on the top floor. Anderson had converted the upper six offices into two apartments. He got a zoning variance because the city didn't really care about the area anymore. I have a residence that has a separate exterior door for the living room, kitchen and the bedroom, the three former offices. Holly Pena and her son, Chris, lived in the other three-doored apartment. Anderson gave it to her for a token rent when he hired her to offset the ridiculously low wages he gave her. Her wages are still low, but no longer "ridiculously" low.

I ate lunch from a combination of take out leftovers—Mexican chicken, pizza and Chinese vegetables. I couldn't find anything on my thirty cable channels, so I watched an old videotape of a basketball semi-final, and found myself silently rooting for a team that had already been eliminated. I watched the eleven o'clock news to see the baseball and basketball scores.

I fell asleep without turning off the television. It was still on when the phone woke me up.

"Mr. Fisher?" the voice said tentatively. When someone calls you up at three in the morning and doesn't use your first name, it's usually bad news.

"Yes?"

"This is Christy Baker. I need your help. Can you come here?"

"Where's here?"

"Seven hundred Wishon. Number nine."

"Give me ten minutes."

I hung up, stood up. Since I still had my clothes on, I was ready to go. I thought about brushing my teeth, but took a drink of warm Diet Pepsi instead. That should kill any lingering germs.

Wishon was a one-way street in that block, going the wrong way in this situation, so I had to take another one-way street past the seven hundred block and then come back down Wishon. The huge house at 700 Wishon had been a large fashionable house at one time. It had probably belonged to one of San Joaquin's old rich, and dated back at least to the twenties. It had since been divided into apartments.

Since I could only see one dim light in the building, I decided that might be number nine. It was.

The light came through a set of multi-paned windowed double doors. One of the squares of glass was broken, the shattered glass lay on the floor just inside the door. I didn't like the looks of this and thought about investing in a gun if I continued in this line of work.

The door was closed but not locked, at least not anymore. I lowered my face to the broken pane and quietly called out Christy's name, softly knocking at the same time. There was no answer, but I went in anyway. I was prepared for something terrible, and that something terrible turned out to be Tom Hammerhill lying face down in the middle of the room. On both sides of his torso, two pools of darkening blood contrasted with the worn lighter-colored hardwood floor.

From behind another door I could hear a faint sobbing. I

assumed it was Christy, but I still went to the door slowly. I pushed the door open carefully. It was the bathroom. The light wasn't on, but as the light from the living room entered the bathroom I could see Christy sitting on the floor against the far wall, her legs tucked up to her chest. She was still making the sobbing sound. Her eyes were closed.

I had walked halfway across the bathroom floor and called her name several times before she opened her eyes to look at me. But these weren't the same eyes from the coffee shop. I figured she was on drugs of some sort. I helped her to her feet. She was wearing only panties and a T-shirt. The panties were the same ones she had on earlier, I recognized the floral pattern. There was something familiar about the T-shirt as well. It was covered in the same dark blood that was hardening on the floor in the other room. Tom Hammerhill's blood.

I had seen blood before. I had seen a dead body before, but it had been twenty-seven years. I held Christy up, trying not to get any blood on myself. She could hardly stand and her eyes kept rolling back into her head. I carried her the three steps to the bathtub, lifted her in and turned on the shower, just the cold water.

The sound she made now was a variation on the sobbing. Not louder, merely different in tone. I left her in the shower and went to the kitchen, passing Tom Hammerhill, who was still dead. Christy had not anticipated the need to sober up quickly. All I could find in the kitchen was decaffeinated coffee and herbal tea. The best I could do was a Coca Cola Classic in the refrigerator.

Back in the shower, Christy had stopped making the sobbing

noise and her eyes were open but extremely glazed and dilated. The water had washed away most of the blood, but the t shirt was permanently stained. I turned off the water and lifted her out of the tub. Sitting her on the toilet, I pulled off the shirt and wrapped her in a towel that was barely large enough to go around her hundred or so pound frame. I leaned her back against the toilet tank. I took the blanket off the bed and wrapped it around her twice.

Christy Baker was a very attractive woman, and it had been some time since I had been this close to a naked woman. Yet there was nothing sexual about it. Maybe a stoned, practically comatose young woman sitting on a toilet didn't turn me on the way it might for some men. Perhaps it was the bloody t shirt I had just removed and the dead body in the next room. Or maybe a combination of both.

I poured some of the Coke into her mouth and she swallowed it. She seemed to be coming around. Although her eyes were open, it took a little while for them to actually focus and look at me with some sign of recognition.

"Fisher?" she said softly and tentatively.

"Yes."

"Oh, Fisher!" she gasped. No more sobbing now. This was full out crying. Big sobs. Big tears. I thought she would hyperventilate or something. I held her close to me. I hadn't been this close to a crying woman in a long time either, but this seemed like the right thing to do.

After a while, I don't know how long, the crying subsided but seemed poised to return at any moment.

"Oh, Fisher," she said. "Tommy's dead."

"Can you tell me about it now?"

"I can't. I need to get out of here."

"You can't. You're in a lot of trouble. There's a dead man in the next room. If you want me to help you, you're going to have to tell me what happened."

"I didn't do it, you know."

"O.K., then tell me who did."

"You don't believe me, do you? You think I killed him, don't you?" That chip on her shoulder edge was returning to her voice. I supposed that was a good sign.

"Listen, there's a guy with a knife in him in the next room. When I got here you were stoned out of your mind and you were covered with his blood. I'm willing to listen to you, but frankly, it doesn't look real good for you at this point."

"They made me do it," she said. "They made me do it"

"Who made you do it?" I asked. "Made you do what?"

"Made me kill Tommy."

"Who are they?"

"Three guys," she answered. "They broke in, and pointed guns at us. Then one of them held me and another one stuck me with a hypodermic needle. Then things went a little fuzzy. The next thing I remember is lying on the floor. One of them put a knife in my hand and then they laid Tommy on top of me, on the knife."

"And that's how he got stabbed?" I asked.

"Yeah."

"Where did the knife come from?"

"I don't know."

"What happened after they made you stab Tommy?"

"I don't know. I woke up with him laying on top of me. Then I called you." she said.

"Do you remember anything about them?"

"There were three of them. They were well dressed in a cheap sort of way."

"Like what?"

"Sports jackets, with open shirts. Polyester. Jewelry. Lots of gold. Cowboy boots."

"Cowboy boots?"

"Yeah, at least one of them was wearing cowboy boots. I saw them when I was on the floor."

"Anything else?"

"They were Mexicans."

"Are you sure?"

"Yes, they were dark, and they spoke Spanish."

"To each other?"

"Yes, and to Tommy."

"To Tommy?

"Tommy spoke fluent Spanish," she said.

"Why me?" I had to ask.

"What do you mean?

"I mean I only met you about twelve hours ago. Then you wake up with a dead man on you and you call me. Not the police, not 911, but me."

"I really don't know anyone else. There's no one else I can

trust."

"I'll take that as a compliment," I said. "You know we're going to have to call the police now, don't you?"

"Do we have to? Can't we just run away?" She was serious.

"If we run, they would come looking for you the minute they found the body. And me, second."

"Why?"

"You're the girlfriend. This is your apartment, that's your T-shirt in the tub covered with blood. And me. It wouldn't take the police long to discover I broke his finger today at lunch. And there were plenty of witnesses who heard me threaten him. I also have something of an exaggerated reputation for violence."

"What can I do?" she asked. "What should I tell the police? They won't believe I didn't kill him. I don't want to go to jail."

The shock was wearing off, and Christy's sense of self-preservation was kicking in. That was a good sign. "Just tell them the truth. It isn't important whether the police believe you or not. It may be a judge and jury that you have to convince," I said, speaking from some experience in that area. "Do you know a good lawyer?"

"No," she said quickly, but then changed her mind. "Yes, I think so."

"When you get to the police station, before you talk to anyone, call him."

"Her."

"What?"

"Her. The lawyer is a woman," she corrected me.

"Just call her when we get there."

"You're going too?"

"They'll probably insist on it," I told her.

Chapter 5

Two policemen arrived at the same time, in separate patrol cars, a mere four minutes after I hung up the phone. I calculated it was about four minutes from the nearest all-night donut shop.

They asked us if we had touched anything, and not to touch anything else. They frisked me and called for a female officer to frisk Christy. They separated us. To prevent us from conferring on our stories, I presume. They guarded us until the detectives arrived, then they continued to guard us. The detectives arrived with an entourage of technicians who looked for fingerprints, took pictures and generally made a mess of the place. Two guys from the coroner's office were standing by with a body bag and a gurney, waiting to take away the late Tom Hammerhill. They were waiting for permission from the person in charge.

The person in charge was one Lt. Frank Sanchez. I had seen him on the television news. Whenever there was a case big enough to make the evening news—not all of them did—Sanchez seemed to be on the scene. That probably meant he was the best the police force had, the guy with the ability to solve the high profile case. It certainly wasn't because he was a fancy dresser. Nor was it his personality.

"Who the fuck are you?" Not the greeting I'm used to.

I told him who I was and even showed him my new private investigator's license. He was shorter than me, but not much, and he was thicker. He seemed wide as a refrigerator, with a box-like physique. He looked uncomfortable in his suit, his wide neck strained at the restriction of his tie.

"Did you get his gun?" he asked my policeman guard.

"I don't have a gun," I said.

"Shut up, I'm not talking to you." He practically spat out the words.

"Did you get his gun?" he said, especially uncivil, to the uniformed officer, who informed him I did not have one.

He looked at me severely. "So we've got a dead body, a drugged-out broad, and a private detective with no gun. What the fuck are you doing here anyway?"

"She called me."

"What's so special about you?"

"Nothing. She just called me. She needed help. I came over, sobered her up and then called you guys."

"Why didn't you call us first?"

"She was pretty far gone. I was afraid she would O.D. or go into a coma."

"How do you know her?"

"She is involved in a case I'm working on."

"What kind of case?"

"I really can't say."

"Don't count on that client privilege bullshit too much. If I want to know, you'll tell me."

Call me overly sensitive, but I took this as a threat. I was trying to think of a snappy private detective type comeback when Sanchez just walked away. Perhaps I'd get quicker with more experience.

Sanchez spoke to another detective, "Get a statement from Sherlock Shithead over there."

Imagine my surprise when the other detective walked over to me. This detective was a round-faced, middle-aged guy named Kaprelian. He didn't bother with a tie or jacket. No one was going to put him on television. He dressed like he worked in an auto parts store.

"Name?"

"Sherlock Shithead?" I answered.

Kaprelian smiled a little, careful not to let Sanchez see him. "The Lieutenant is in a bad mood."

"If I hang around with him much longer," I said, "I think my feelings might get hurt."

"He's got a few rough edges, but he's good at his job," Kaprelian informed me.

"That's a relief," I said. "I'd hate to think he was an incompetent asshole."

Kaprelian smiled again, furtively, and then decided to get down to business. “Name?”

When I told him, a flash of recognition traveled across his face. “You’re the Bob Fisher who...”

“Yeah.”

“The TV preacher?”

“Yeah.”

I told him the story of my day, leaving out only the part of who I was working for. I told him about the incident at the coffee shop and Hammerhill’s finger.

“So maybe you and little Christy are doing the dirty deed and the boyfriend comes home and either you or the girl shanks the poor guy.”

“Yeah, we had to kill him because he found out about our connections with Jimmy Hoffa, the Manson Family and the Kennedy assassination,” I said.

“I took a shot,” Kaprelian admitted. “I’m a romantic. I prefer crimes of passion.”

I told Kaprelian the story the way Christy had told it to me.

“I wish it was Jimmy Hoffa instead. We’d have a better chance of catching him than we do these guys,” Kaprelian said. “If there are any such guys,” he added, exhibiting a suspicious side to his nature. “You’re going to need to go downtown with us,” Kaprelian said. “Wait here until we’re done.”

The little army of police technicians went about their work while I sat outside on the steps. One of the officers that arrived first stood near me the whole time. I assume he had been told to keep an eye on me. Other cops woke up residents in the building and next door. None of them had heard anything. Eventually a full black body bag the size of Tommy Hammerhill was wheeled out, put in the back of a black station wagon with "Coroner" painted on the side. I thought about body bags for a moment.

"Now we're all going downtown," Kaprelian announced as he followed the body out. "Of course, he's going to the basement and we're going to the second floor."

"Should I follow you in my car?" I asked.

"No way," Kaprelian said. "I don't really think you did this but why take a chance that you'll skip out. You'll ride with me."

"Can I play with the siren?"

I didn't get to play with the siren, but Kaprelian used the flashing lights at the intersections so he wouldn't have to wait for the light to change, confirming a long held suspicion of mine that cops weren't always in a big hurry when they did that.

The traffic in downtown San Joaquin was about average for four-thirty in the morning, that is, virtually nonexistent. Kaprelian parked in the underground garage under the police station. On the other side of the garage, I could see the coroner's wagon with the back door open. Tommy Hammerhill had gotten here before I did. I hoped I wouldn't have to be here any longer than him.

Upstairs I was asked to wait in an uncomfortable wooden chair and offered a cup of coffee, which I declined. I don't like coffee and I was as awake as I wanted to be. Christy arrived after a while, accompanied by a uniformed female officer. She was freshly dressed, but her hair, now dry, was still uncombed. The only color in her face was her blood.

She stepped away from her escort as they neared where I was sitting and she spoke softly, not so much that she didn't want anyone to hear, rather, that was all the strength she could muster at that time. "Thank you for helping me," she said. "I don't know what..."

"That's all right. You know you don't have to say anything without a lawyer. Did you call one yet?"

"Not yet."

"They owe you a phone call. Use it."

The officer motioned for her to go and they went into another room together. Eventually I was asked to repeat my story into a tape recorder with Kaprelian and another plainclothes cop in the room. After that, I returned to the wooden chair and sat until Kaprelian came out and said, "You can go."

I reminded him that my car was back at Christy's apartment. This got a big laugh out of his big round face. He handed me fifty cents. "We're kind of busy around here right now. Take the bus, would you?" Another big laugh.

I let him walk away without informing him that the bus fare was seventy-five cents now, and that the buses didn't even start running for another forty-five minutes. I kept the fifty cents, though.

As I was leaving, I saw Christy emerge from the room she went in earlier. Only now she was accompanied by a sharply dressed young man carrying a briefcase. They were followed by another sharply dressed man with a briefcase and an equally sharply dressed woman. She didn't have a briefcase. I decided the one that didn't have to carry a briefcase must be the leader.

I had seen enough lawyers in my life to recognize the species. These weren't your average, run-of-the-mill public defenders or ambulance chasers. These guys weren't in the league with Cooper Page, either. This particular breed traveled in packs and probably seldom saw a police station this close, especially at this time of day. These guys didn't advertise on television. They looked like they just stepped out of the latest issue of a lawyer fashion magazine—there probably is such a publication. Standing next to Sanchez they looked like a visual aid on how to wear a suit and how not to wear a suit. These were the kind of lawyers that made cops with attitudes, like Sanchez and Kaprelian, stand up straight and toe the line. Sanchez was sweating through his cheap suit as they accompanied Christy out of there. They all marched right by me looking neither to the right or to the left, but straight ahead.

Christy, too. Not a word. And after all we'd been through together.

A Mercedes the size of a cruise ship was pulling away from the front of police headquarters as I came out the front door. I can only assume that Christy thought I brought my own car.

I walked across the street to the Dia del Luz—which means "light of day," I think, an establishment frequented mostly by cops, freshly released prisoners, transients, and other denizens of the night. The all night eatery was a San Joaquin institution, in the same location for almost seventy years. The original owners were gone, but the new owners had mastered the art of blending cheap meat, grease and starch into just the right combinations to satisfy the discriminating palates of their devoted clientele.

I ordered my favorite, *chorizo con huevos*. Eggs scrambled with a spicy Mexican sausage of questionable ingredients. It came with a huge side of greasy potatoes and tortillas. I washed it down with a large Diet Pepsi and ate undisturbed except for an obviously homeless man who asked for a quarter so he could go to Modesto. I gave him the fifty cents Kaprelian had given me without a word.

The buses were running now. I took seventy-five cents of my own and used it to take the number 28, north along Van Ness.

The passengers, mostly Hispanics and Southeast Asians—that's who lived in central San Joaquin—were on their way to work in the stores and shops of North San Joaquin, or to school at San Joaquin High or San Joaquin City College, or, if they transferred buses, to the state university farther north. The city was moving north and leaving the downtown and most of the people on this bus behind.

The ride to the Tower District wasn't that long, and the bus dropped me off near my building. I walked upstairs and reassumed my position on the couch.

Chapter 6

The phone woke me up again. It was eight a.m. if you could believe the digital clock on the VCR, which I immediately did not. I thought about not answering it, but picked it up anyway.

"Mr. Fisher?"

There was that "Mister" again. "Yes?"

"This is C. Thomas Baker." Said as if that meant something.

"O. K."

"I am Christina's father."

"Christina who?"

"Christina Baker," he said, his voice growing indignant for some reason.

"Listen, I don't know any Christina Baker...

"Christy," he interrupted. "Christy Baker."

"Oh, Christy," I said as some more of my brain woke up. "Yes, we had a very interesting morning."

"That's what I would like to talk to you about," he said. "How soon do you think you could get here?"

"That depends on where here is, I suppose."

"Van Ness Extension, past Herndon on the Bluffs."

"There's no telling," I said. "I haven't had much sleep. Perhaps you could come to my office later this afternoon."

"I'd like to straighten out this mess as soon as possible. Christy is here. She and her mother are fairly distraught. I don't think I should leave them alone. I'm not even going to the office today."

What a great dad, choosing to stay home with his daughter just because she is involved in a murder.

"Well, I'll try to get there as soon as I can," I said unenthusiastically.

He gave me the exact address and added: "You would be paid for your time, of course."

Of course.

My shower was a little shorter than I would have liked. I shaved and put on my best, most expensive casual clothes. I passed on the suit and tie. It wasn't even noon yet and it was already one hundred degrees, a typical spring day in San Joaquin.

None of my cars had air conditioning. As I pointed it north, I guessed that it would soon be the only 1966 Dodge Dart on Van Ness Extension.

From its founding, the most prestigious residential street in the city of San Joaquin was Van Ness Boulevard. The homes of the rich and powerful slowly migrated north over the years. Some of the fine houses have been lost to time, urban redevelopment, and the overall decay and abandonment of the downtown area. In the thirties and forties, another Van Ness Boulevard was built with large expensive homes. The fact that the two Van Ness Boulevards were not even connected did not seem unusual to anyone apparently. When that strip was completely developed another Van Ness Boulevard appeared beginning about four miles east of where the second Van Ness Boulevard ended. The City, in this case to avoid confusion, called this one Van Ness Extension. This particular Van Ness was populated by San Joaquin's new rich, real estate developers, retail moguls, doctors, lawyers.

In the first half of the century what is now Van Ness Extension was this country's primary source of figs. In fact, the area is historically referred to as Fig Garden. Contemporary real estate agents will attach the label Fig Garden as they attach a higher price. One would be hard pressed to find very many fig trees around here today though.

Driving north, I managed to take all three Van Nesses. The Dart's mileage odometer numbers got higher at a slower rate than the increase in real estate values. The farther north I traveled, the more showy and ostentatious the houses became. Tudor mansions, Mediterranean Villas, Southern Colonials, pseudo-Victorians, all in a row.

At the end of Van Ness Extension was the generally dry San Joaquin River. The bluffs overlooking the river bed was now the premier residential location in the city. In the flat San Joaquin Valley, there are no panoramic views. On a clear day, one could see the Sierra Nevada Mountains to the northeast, but increasing smog and the traditional winter fog, made such days more infrequent. That left a meandering cottonwood and valley oak-lined strip of sand with an occasional trickle of water to qualify as a vista. So now, after taking some of the world's finest fruit growing acreage out of production, the rich were encroaching on the last bit of natural habitat left in the San Joaquin Valley.

As much as I resent the loss of agriculture and nature, there was a part of me that knew, if my numbers came up in the lottery, I would be out here in a minute.

The residence of C. Thomas Baker and family was at the end of Van Ness Extension where it reached the river. The house was a re-creation of an English Tudor. It was surrounded by a re-creation of an elaborate English garden populated by trees, shrubs and plants as foreign to the Central California heat and perennial drought conditions as penguins in Palm Springs. I drove up to the driveway gate, not sure what to do. There was a closed circuit television camera and an intercom. I didn't know whether to wave or order a Big Mac. A static, disembodied voice came over the intercom and completed by fast food drive through metaphor. "Can I help you?" it said. A million dollar house and a two dollar intercom.

"Bob Fisher to see Mr. Baker."

A moment passed. I expected the voice to ask me if I wanted fries. "You're expected," the voice informed me.

A metallic click was followed by the double doors of the gate slowly swinging open. I drove the Dart through and saw them close in the rear view mirror. I parked as close to the front door as the circular driveway would allow, wondering whether there was a service entrance which I should use.

I took a chance on the front door. Doors, actually. Double doors. It opened as I approached it. Actually only one of them opened. I'd always wondered about double doors. They might be real handy when it came to moving something in or out, but the average sized person only requires one to enter or exit. I guess it was just for effect.

The door was opened by a man in a suit. "Mr. Baker?" I assumed. Wrongly.

"Mr. and Mrs. Baker are in the solarium," he said.

A servant. It was the guy whose voice I heard over the intercom. I was wrong again. It wasn't that the intercom sounded bad, it was that his voice did.

I followed him over polished hardwood floors through a hall that separated large, ornate rooms with high ceiling and museum-like furnishings. That was the impression I got from the place, that of a museum. It didn't feel like anybody actually lived here. Of course, with three people, spread over ten thousand square feet of living space, maybe it was hard to establish much of a "homey" feeling. The house was cool compared to the outside. I'm glad the walk was long. It gave the wet spot on my back a chance to dry before I met the rest of the Baker family.

The solarium was at the back of the house. It was a large room virtually made of windows. It was like a greenhouse with wicker furniture. There were about a million plants, ferns and small palms. A fountain at the center fed a small brook which flowed into the swimming pool. The Bakers had chosen to eliminate altogether that tedious walk from the house to the pool by having the pool come right into the solarium. The glass came down to water level, dividing the pool equally between outdoors and indoors. The divider could apparently be raised and lowered to facilitate swimming laps or to open the solarium to the outdoors. It was currently closed, a concession to the triple digit temperatures. It was very comfortable in here now.

The butler announced me. "Mr. Fisher." I'm glad that's all he needed to say. I'm sure his voice could get on your nerves after a while.

Mr. Baker rose from his white wicker chair and extended his hand for me to shake. I walked over and shook it. We were about the same size. My basketball experience makes me tend to judge people according to size, giving me some basic idea of how I will do against them. The idea is that I have the advantage of size and strength over a smaller person and quickness over a larger one. It's not the best way to judge a person, of course, and often proved totally wrong on the basketball court, as well as in life. Mr. Baker seemed to be doing the same thing. When he seemed sure his grip was firmer than mine, he released my hand and motioned towards another wicker chair.

I don't know if these were his best casual clothes, but they looked better than mine. His pants were well creased and his polo shirt looked fresh, crisp and new. He wore deck shoes with no socks, a practice I give up this time of year because the heat made the leather against your sweaty skin like walking in a swamp after a while.

"This is my wife, Cecilia," he said, referring to the semi-prone woman in a chaise lounge. She raised the glass of whatever she was drinking in what was either a toast or a wave. The glass contained something the color of iced tea, but iced tea was usually served in a taller glass.

I nodded back since I didn't have a glass to return her toast. "Good afternoon," I said, even though I wasn't sure if it truly was yet. Long mornings with corpses and police distorted my sense of time.

"Could we get you something to eat? Perhaps you would like something to drink?" Baker asked as I sat down. I was still burping up the *chorizo con huevos* from this morning, so I declined the offer of food. "I could use a cold drink," I said. "Some iced tea or a diet soda."

"Nash," Baker said, the reason for which I couldn't figure out until the butler moved toward a small refrigerator. The butler's name was Nash.

Nash quickly had a tumbler full of soda with ice, carbonation still fizzing in front of me on a tray. I took it off the tray and took a sip. It was Diet Coke. I can tell.

There was an awkward silence. Mr. and Mrs. Baker were both staring at me. I didn't know whether they were waiting for me to fall over dead or say something. I chose to say something trite. "Pretty hot out there," I said, and took another sip.

"Yes," he said. "It's a tropical depression. It really increases the humidity. There should be a break in this weather system soon, though."

That was more than I wanted to know about the weather. It was always hot in San Joaquin during the summer. The variations didn't interest me. Nor did it interest Mrs. Baker very much, though she continued to smile, probably more as a result of the drink she was finishing than pride over her husband's meteorological expertise. It seemed her robe was either shrinking or getting shorter. A latent chauvinist impulse made me wonder if she was wearing anything under the robe.

"This is very pleasant, sitting around drinking soda and chatting about the weather," I said, "but I had the impression you wanted to see me about what happened with Christy last night, or this morning actually."

"Right to the point. I like that," he said. If he liked it so much, why didn't he get to it? "Christy is our only child, and, let's face it, she's never wanted for anything. You could say we've spoiled her, but we like to think we're just generous. We didn't think too much of it when she got involved with this Eternal Truth Temple thing. We thought it was just a phase. You know, a young person looking to find herself. But when she said she wasn't going to college and she moved up in the mountains to join that cult, well, you can imagine our distress."

I imagined.

"Then after a while," he continued, "she saw the error of her decisions, and came to see the cult and those two buffoons for what they really were. Of course, nothing we could say would ever sway her."

Of course.

"Then she joined that Committee against the Church. We'd wished she just would have put the whole thing behind her and move on with her life. However, a psychiatrist friend suggested we humor her work with the Committee. Said it would be therapeutic. I suppose it was. She had to deal with the public and the press and she handled it very well. She was doing very well in school, if you want to call a community college a school. Well, at least she will be able to transfer to a decent school. Her decision to live in that ghetto and cohabit with that Hammerhill low-life added to our apprehension and distress."

There was that word "distress" again. I was distressed over his characterization of the Tower District as a ghetto. I lived in that neighborhood as well. Not to mention his distressful attitude about California's fine community college system.

"And now she's involved in a murder," he reminded me. "Well, Mr. Fisher, you can see our distress."

"Distress" again.

"So I would like to hire you to help straighten out this mess."

"That's very flattering and all," I said. "But I already have a client and one is about all I can handle. From what I can tell, that legal army of yours should be able to straighten out this mess. If they can't, they should all be shot." A slight hyperbole for effect, though not entirely a bad concept. "Christy's story is too bizarre to be completely made up. So you've got drugs, a religious cult, and Mexicans. All that should add up to reasonable doubt in this city, and that's all Christy needs."

"Are you saying you won't help us?" Baker asked.

"No, what I'm saying is that I won't work for you. If I happen to learn anything that might help Christy, I'll pass it along."

"You see, Mr. Fisher, I just want to do everything possible to get her out of this situation. I'm sure you can appreciate our distress over this matter."

There's that word again.

"Yes, I can," I said. "But it could be worse."

"How's that?"

"You could be Tommy Hammerhill's parents."

We had another one of those uncomfortable silences. We all looked at each other for a moment. "I was wondering if I could see Christy before I left?" I asked.

"I think that would be all right," Mr. Baker said.

"Nash, show Mr. Fisher to Christy's room."

"Follow me, please," Nash said, as we took a different tour of the Baker Museum of Conspicuous Consumption. We went upstairs where he knocked at a closed door. Christy didn't answer. The door was opened by a woman, probably a nurse, hired by the Bakers. They spoke inaudibly and then the door closed. I thought the nurse had refused to let me in, but then the door opened a moment later.

"Hello, Fisher," Christy said. Her bedroom was as big as my whole apartment. In fact, it had a complete living room set, TV and stereo in it as well as the bed. Christy was sitting on the sofa in one of those short silk robes apparently favored by the Baker females.

"How are you doing?" I asked.

"I've felt better," she said. She'd looked better, too. She was pale and weak looking. She wasn't wearing any make up and the only color in her face was supplied by her bloodshot eyes and the dark circles under them. "Thank you for helping me last night," she said. "They tell me I might have died or something if you hadn't..."

"That's all right," I said awkwardly. "It was nothing." I felt as stupid saying it as it sounded.

"You met my parents?"

"Yes."

"They're not handling this too well," Christy said. "But then, who could?"

She got up from the sofa and walked around, not to anywhere. She just walked around. "We don't get along too well. Never have, really. I'm something of an embarrassment to them. And now with all this..." Her voice just trailed off to nowhere. "I wish I could get out of here."

"It's probably best to stay here, at least until this is all straightened out. It might look better and your father has the resources to help you."

"Did he hire you?"

"He asked but I had to turn him down. I told him there wasn't much I could do anyway."

"I'll tell him to pay you for last night," she said.

"Forget it," I said. "We'll just call it even."

"Even for what?"

"For lying to you. For not telling you I was working for Yogi and Boo-Boo."

She laughed weakly. "That's what we used to call them." She must have meant her and Tommy, because she went silent for a moment.

"I am looking for the sacred computer disc, or whatever. I don't give a damn about their church, or their whole army of airport nuisances. I'm just looking to return some stolen property. I'm new at all this. I'm sorry I had to lie to you."

She was still silent. Finally, she said, "I didn't tell you the whole truth either. I'm pretty sure Tommy was either involved in stealing the disc or knew something about it."

"Why do you think that?"

"Not long after our meeting after the coffee shop, he made a phone call to someone. He seemed nervous and angry at the same time."

"What did he say?"

"I'm not sure. He was speaking Spanish."

"So you wouldn't understand?"

"Yes, I think so," she said. "Maybe he was trying to protect me."

"Why do you think he was talking about the disc?"

"Well, some words in Spanish sound like they do in English," she explained. "Computer disc in Spanish is something like *computador disco* or *disco computador*, or something like that. Also he said something like 'just boot it up.' He said that in English like he didn't know how to say 'boot it' in Spanish."

"Boot it?"

"You know, 'boot it'? Boot the disc?"

I was confused and it showed.

"You don't know much about computers, do you?"

I shook my head no. We had a computer at the office, but Holly was the only one that ever touched it.

"'Boot it' means to put a disc in the drive and then turn on the computer. Then you can bring whatever data that's on the disc up on the screen."

"Could he have been talking to someone else from the Committee?"

"Not likely," she said. "There's not very many of us in the first place, and no one besides Tommy can speak Spanish that I know of."

"Is there anyone else that might know something? Someone with the Committee maybe?"

"The only other people in San Joaquin that are in the Committee are Peter Rawson and Angie Fernandes. But they've pretty much dropped out of the Committee. They're still around somewhere, but I don't know where."

"I'll find them," I said. "After all, I am a detective." There I go again, not telling the whole truth.

I did have a file folder on both of them. "Well, I hope this works out for you. It should. Maybe I'll be seeing you around sometime." I felt like a nervous teenager saying goodbye on a first date. I needed to go but I didn't know how to get out of the room. Christy helped. She got up from the couch and walked over to me. The robe was very short.

She walked up to me and hugged me, tightly. “Thank you,” she said. I hugged her back softly. I knew I had better leave now.

“So long,” I said, and walked to the door.

Nash and the nurse had disappeared and I was left to find my own way out. I walked back to the solarium to say goodbye to Mr. and Mrs. Baker, not something I wanted to do, but something that I felt social and professional etiquette called for.

I walked into the room. Mrs. Baker was finishing whatever was in her glass. I didn’t know whether this was the same drink or how many more she had consumed in my absence.

“I just wanted to say goodbye,” I said.

“You just missed Thomas,” she informed me. “He had to go to the office before he had withdrawal symptoms.” She laughed at her little joke, and then stood up. She and her daughter were quite similar. “Thank you for coming,” she said. I thought she was going to walk over and hug me as well, but she merely walked to the edge of the pool. She kept her eyes on mine as she dipped her toe into the water to test the temperature of the water. It must have been satisfactory, because she then unfastened the robe and let it drop to the floor.

My curiosity about what was under the robe was answered. Nothing. She was wearing nothing at all. She watched my eyes as they wandered up and down her body. She liked to be looked at. She had put a lot of time and money to maintain that body. Later I wondered if medical technology kept those breasts and buttocks so high. I wasn't thinking about that at the time, though.

She turned her back to me and stepped down onto the first step, then turned back to face me again.

"Have a nice day," I said, and walked out. Nash was nowhere around, so I saw myself out. The gate opened by itself as I approached it and closed behind me as I turned south on Van Ness Extension. It was hot. I was sweating.

Chapter 7

Peter Rawson lived near San Joaquin State University. Since I was already on the north side of town, I thought I'd look in on him. It was hot, but it wasn't going to get any cooler, so what the hell. I drove east past the fast food places, shopping malls, and offices toward the university.

When I first moved to San Joaquin, the college, not even a university then, was considered way out in the country. The School of Agriculture built its farm, complete with goats, sheep, chickens, cattle and pigs, along with fruits and vegetables of every kind. Now the city had surrounded the university and its farm, and some residents were petitioning to have the farm removed. Animals and manure and fertilizer were now a nuisance, instead of the selling point that brought the developers out here in the first place. It's just another urban sprawl story. They're pretty common in California. Like people who move near an airport which has been there for fifty years and all of a sudden start complaining about the noise. What did they expect living near an airport—or a farm, for that matter—would be like?

Rawson lived in an area that used to be called "Sin City." It was a square block made up of crowded apartment buildings and complexes, originally built for the college students. It was called "Sin City" because of the alleged wild lifestyle of students in the sixties and seventies. As the buildings deteriorated and more housing options opened up for students in the area, Sin City was gradually abandoned by the college crowd and replaced by more of a welfare crowd. The recent influx of Southeast Asian refugees to San Joaquin has turned the area into an Asian ghetto, an island of poverty and squalor bordered by the university and some of the city's prime residential and business areas.

It was now sometimes called "Little Saigon." That was a misnomer. It would more accurately be called "Little Phnom Penh" or "Little Vientene," since most of the residents were Cambodian or Laotian, not Vietnamese. The Asians tended to be lumped together as if one entity by those who happened to get here before they did. The racial slurs "gook" and "slant" were making a comeback.

I parked the Dart on the street where it fit in with the other battered autos of the area. I searched the maze of crowded two-story buildings for Rawson's apartment. The numbers didn't seem to have any real pattern. The lawns were dead or worn away to dirt. The area was littered with paper and broken toys. Doors and windows were generally open. Barefoot Asian children ran around everywhere. Exotic music and the smell of garlic and unknown foods drifted from the open apartments.

I found Rawson's building. It was on the ground floor. I knocked on the hollow-core door. The television was on, but was turned down when I knocked. The door was full of pinholes from tacking notes to it. Either that, or it had been used as a backboard for a dart game. I knocked again.

Sensing that I wasn't going to go away, Rawson eventually opened the door. The delay hadn't been from him dressing, or even bathing. He was wearing gym shorts and a torn T-shirt, both of which looked and smelled as though they were recently salvaged from the bottom of his dirty clothes hamper. I walked in, uninvited, and immediately reconsidered that clothes hamper theory. It seemed evident he didn't have one. Clothes and towels, not to mention paper, bottles and cans, were strewn about the room. The room was furnished in a minimalist style, with only a small television and a bare mattress, bent and propped up against a wall to serve as a couch. This place was a definite contrast to the Baker house.

"Hey, you can't come in here!" he said, unconvincingly.

"I'm already in, aren't I? Christy Baker sent me."

"I don't know any Christy Baker," he lied.

"She knows you," I said. "She said you might know something about a missing computer disc that belongs to the Eternal Truth Temple."

"I don't know anything about any disc or any Church."

"I'm sure," I said, "that there are a great many things that you don't know about—soap for one—but you do know about the

Temple. I have seen their file on you. And you do know Christy Baker because you worked for the Committee."

"I don't know what you're talking about," he insisted.

"I suppose the name Tommy Hammerhill doesn't ring a bell either then?"

"Never heard of him."

"Then it wouldn't make any difference to you to know that he is dead."

"Tommy's dead? How?"

"This is a surprising bit of concern for someone you don't know."

"How did he die?"

"So you did know him, then?"

"Just tell me what happened to Tommy?"

"He was murdered and Christy Baker got framed for it.,

"Is she in jail?"

"More concern about people you don't know. How compassionate. No, her father bailed her out. She thinks it might have something to do with the missing disc. What do you think?"

"I don't know."

"Do you speak Spanish?"

"What?"

"Do you speak Spanish?"

"No. Why?"

"The people that killed Tommy spoke Spanish. Sound like anyone you know?"

"This is San Joaquin, California. A lot of people speak

Spanish."

"Yes, but they all don't kill people," I said. "You sure you don't know anything about the missing disc, or anything that could help Christy?"

"Fuck you!"

I thought about punching the scrawny punk in the nose, but instead gave him one of my cards. "Call me if you happen to think of anything." I stepped gingerly toward the door, trying not to step on, or in, anything. I didn't look back when Rawson slammed the door behind me.

Chapter 8

I purposely drove past where I should turn to return to the office. I drove downtown to the main county library, found a parking space with over an hour left on the meter. The library was fairly crowded. It was air conditioned, so there were a lot of older people there who probably didn't have air conditioning, or couldn't afford to run it all the time. They were sitting around reading, or just sitting around. The library was also frequented by a few homeless people who came in to use the rest room, or get out of the heat. They would pick up a book, find a semi-comfortable chair and take a nap.

I went to the reference section. All those years of college and all those degrees might be of some value in my new career after all. I knew what I wanted, but it took me a while to find it. A few years ago, I would have looked in a variety of reference books and indexes, or the Reader's Guide to Periodical Literature. Now everything was on computer. This was supposed to save time, but not being technologically oriented, it probably worked out to take as long. Actually all I had to do was follow some simple onscreen instructions, then type in Eternal Truth Temple. After that, I pressed the "print" key and four pages of information rolled up out of the printer.

The information listed articles and books on the Yogi and the Baba and the Temple. The library hadn't progressed so much, however, that I didn't have to fill out a little slip for each article and then wait twenty minutes for a librarian to go into the basement and bring up the two dozen or so periodicals.

California has a long experience with strange cults and sects, fringe religions and eccentric communities. The most heterogeneous of the states, there has always been a tradition of tolerance. At the end of the westward migration, it has always seemed only natural that the unorthodox would end up here with no place further to go.

Aimee Semple McPherson pioneered "religious" broadcasting in the 20s in L.A., and also pioneered the concept of sexual scandal in the field. The Krishnamurti Sect have been in Ojai since 1920. The Hare Krishnas founded a community in Box Canyon in 1949. The Esalen Institute has been operating near Big Sur on the central coast since the 30s. The Rosicrucians, who date back to Europe in the 1600s, have the headquarters of their international organization located in San Jose.

More recently, California has spawned Synanon, Scientology, est, and Jim Jones and the People's Temple (of Jonestown fame). In Orange County, broadcast evangelists exist alongside

Disneyland and Knott's Berry Farm, and market themselves in much the same way as their theme park neighbors. The latest craze are these "New Age" things—crystals, channeling, past lives therapy and the like.

When the librarian finally returned with the material I requested, I found that most of the articles were brief and didn't tell me much I didn't already know. There were articles about the development of the Temple, from its earliest days in the Bay Area to its present "empire" status. There was a pictorial article on the Temple's development of its headquarters in the Sierra Nevadas, just northeast of San Joaquin. The article was quite positive in tone, and was actually flattering to the Temple, repeatedly stressing the differences between the Eternal Truth Temple and such "evil" religious cults as Jim Jones, the Rajneesh, even Synanon, all of which were getting what you could call "bad press" at the time the article was written.

There were several articles about the Temple's success in its work with ex-convicts and its drug rehabilitation program and its work with the poor in Latin America.

There was a synopsis of the Temple's beliefs which essentially sounded as if they attached a food processor to the word processor, added selected pieces of Kahil Gibran, the Bible, the Koran, Dianetics, the Upanishads, Pascal's Penses, and a healthy dose of fortunes from Chinese fortune cookies, then pressed the "blend" button and the sacred text came out of the printer.

There was also a one-page article in a local magazine about a small weekly newspaper published up in Mariposa County. It seems the editor was run out of Oregon by the Rajneesh and his people, and moved south to settle in California near Yosemite. When the Eternal Truth Temple moved in nearby, in a mood of *deja vu*, he expressed concern that the Temple could pose the same kind of threat to the local community that the Rajneesh did in Oregon.

There was an article about the Yogi and Baba's past. The Yogi, it seemed, was born one Bobby Tatino. He led a nomadic early life with his engineer father, attended the University of Nevada-Las Vegas. Baba/Bobby had a business career before turning to the spiritual life. He sold waterbeds, cars, real estate in Nevada, California, and Arizona, respectively, before joining a small young computer and electronics company in the Silicon Valley.

The Yogi, originally Anthony Yohman, lived as a child in the Panama Canal Zone. He was accepted to the U.S. Coast Guard Academy after high school and spent six years in the service as a helicopter pilot. Upon his discharge he ended up at the same firm as Bobby/Baba in San Jose.

And the rest, as they say, is history.

I made a copy of the articles, returned the stack of magazines to the reference counter. I read the sports pages of the San Joaquin, San Francisco, and Los Angeles papers before I felt as though I was ready to face the heat again.

When I stepped outside, it was like stepping into a dry sauna. The time/temperature sign on the top of San Joaquin Savings matched except for the colon. It was 1:06 and 106 degrees.

The parking meter had expired, but there was no ticket. Perhaps the parking police were only ticketing cars in the shade. Or maybe they just melted. It was even hotter inside the car, a small example of the greenhouse effect at work. I made a vow to punch out the next person who said something like, "Yeah, but there's no humidity."

Chapter 9

The office doors and windows were all open when I pulled up in front of the building. That could mean only one of two things. The office was being painted, or the air conditioning wasn't working. I really hoped Holly had decided to redecorate, maybe brighten up those drab office walls.

When I saw Holly sitting between two fans without a paint brush in her hand, I knew it was the air conditioning. "They'll be out this evening," she said.

"How can you be sure?" I asked, skeptical through many years of experience with service people.

"I told them I would throw in some collection work if they'd do it today," she said. She then thought perhaps her free handed manner with the company needed some explanation. "That's the way Mr. Anderson always worked things out. He would..."

"I know. It's all right," I said to reassure her. "You did the right thing." I might have been the boss now, but Holly had pretty much run things for years, even before Anderson died. If she ever left, I'd have to burn down the building for the insurance, but then she was the only one who knew where the policy was.

That was the way Anderson did things, too. He would often barter service for service, or merchandise for service. The cash flow was often minimal, but everything in the building worked, we had good computers and supplies in the office and decent appliances—microwaves, televisions, refrigerators—upstairs in the apartments.

Anderson, I believe, only added the "Investigation" to the firm to give the "Collection" part a little more psychological clout, thinking the "threat" of a private investigator would encourage the payment of delinquent bills.

That was also how the Anderson Collections and Investigations came to possess three finely tuned used cars, a VW Dasher, a Chevy pickup, and the Dart. Anderson tracked down some slow loan payers and repossessed cars for used car dealers who gave him a car as payment. That was the way Anderson worked, and Holly was keeping that tradition alive.

"Let's go to Yosemite," I suggested suddenly.

"What?"

"Let's go to Yosemite," I repeated. "Close the office, drive to Yosemite, get something to eat, look around, you know?"

"What about all this work?"

"It can wait. Turn on the answering machine. We can be there in an hour."

"It's 85 miles," Holly said.

"O.K., an hour and a half. Besides, I'm sure the heat would detrimentally affect your production efficiency, or something."

"I don't know."

"Come on, we'll take my car."

She rolled her eyes. "No, we'll take my car. It has Chris' car seat in it already and it has air conditioning."

"Let's go, Chris," I called to Chris in the next room. "We're going to the mountains."

"Why?" he asked.

"Because it is very beautiful and it is cooler there."

"Why?" he said again.

"Because..." I didn't know what to say. I looked to Holly for help. By this time she had turned off her fans, and turned on the answering machine.

"Lock the door," she said, "and don't forget to turn on the alarm. I'll go get Chris' stuff and meet you at the car. Chris, clean up your mess before we leave."

We both did what we were told and were waiting by Holly's Honda Accord when she came down. "Are you sure you set the alarm?"

"Of course," I said. "Can we go now?"

She strapped Chris into the child's safety seat in the back. He was getting a little big for it. "Do you want me to drive?" I asked.

"No, it's my car. I'll drive."

We got in and she refused to start the car or turn on the air conditioning until I buckled up. "Why do you have a better car than I do?" I asked her.

"It's simple. I went down to the dealer, made a deal, then went to the credit union, borrowed the money, gave it to the dealer, and now I pay the credit union every month. That's how I got this car. It could work for you, too. You should try it sometime."

Chris was asleep in the back before we got to the first light. A car ride was like a sedative for Chris. He was five years old, almost six. Holly was twenty-two. Simple arithmetic says she was barely seventeen when Chris was born, sixteen when she got pregnant. She seldom spoke of her pre-Chris, pre-Anderson Collections and Investigation life, but from what Anderson told me and what little I managed to glean from Holly, it wasn't pleasant. She was not so much abused as ignored as a child, perhaps that is why she now lavished so much attention on Chris. With no encouragement, she didn't do well in school. She hardly attended her first two years of high school, falling in with the omnipresent "bad" crowd. She got pregnant by a boy who has either vanished from the face of the earth, or just doesn't care. Her parents threw her out and she went to live with a cousin in the projects. She went on welfare, had the baby, and seemed destined for the teenage welfare mother life.

The birth of Chris seemed to change Holly's life, though. Instead of going back to high school and being three years behind, she took the California High School Proficiency Test and passed it. Passing the test gave her the equivalent of a high school diploma and allowed her to enter San Joaquin City College. She took advantage of every program the state, county and college had that were designed for low-income, welfare, single parent,

Hispanic women. She parleyed her college grants, welfare, food stamps and the college's free day care into an independent life of her own. She got her own apartment and was doing well in school.

That's how Anderson "found" her. He needed someone to work in the office part time, and city college had a work study program that placed needy students in jobs, whose wages were partially paid by the state. Anderson particularly liked not paying all of Holly's wages. When the work study program was eliminated, Anderson discovered that he, and the company, couldn't do without her, so he hired her full-time, though still for way less than she was worth, gave her flexible hours, and the apartment. As Anderson Collections prospered—almost singly due to Holly's computer expertise—she has since traded in on the Honda, and a basic health insurance plan.

When Anderson died and left it to me, I told Holly she was free to handle the business in whatever way she saw fit—she had a B.A. in Business Administration by this time. She increased our profit by 250 percent in the first year, all by computer generated mailings. We never actually have to go out and collect anything anymore. Our computer merely threatens to ruin their credit for life, seize their assets, put a lien on their property, etc. It works. It makes enough money for Holly to go to graduate school for her MBA, give her a substantial raise, and for me to play private investigator and to close the office and drive to Yosemite.

She drove east on Belmont past small Asian grocery stores, two tortilla factories, and empty storefronts until she hit the freeway.

San Joaquin has a couple of freeways and more on the way. However, when someone says the "freeway," they're usually talking about Freeway 41. If they say the "highway," they are talking about Highway 99. That's just the way it is in San Joaquin.

Freeway 41's official name is the Dwight D. Eisenhower Memorial Freeway, named after the president in office when it was first designed. The freeway, as it is today, came into existence during the Reagan administration. Efforts to call it the Eisenhower Freeway or even the "Ike Pike" essentially fizzled out. So it's just called "41" or "the freeway." And it's really only a freeway through the city of San Joaquin. On the rest of its path through central California, from coastal San Luis Obispo to the Sierra Nevadas and Yosemite, it is merely a two-lane country road.

We had reached that point, at the San Joaquin River, where the six lanes suddenly bottlenecks into two. We crossed the river into Madera County, the road free of the mountain-dweller city-worker commuters and relatively free of the Yosemite bound train of campers and RVs. Most of the million plus visitors to Yosemite took the 41 route and pass through San Joaquin, "the Gateway to Yosemite," which is not to be confused with the other "Gateways to Yosemite" such as Madera, Merced, and Manteca.

The Honda left the valley behind and climbed and turned effortlessly through the curves of the foothills. It was still hot outside, but the air conditioning kept it away from us. We passed through the tiny village of Coarsegold and minutes later had reached the larger town of Oakhurst and its "Gateway to Yosemite" sign. We stopped at a market. I gave Holly $20 and told her that the basic food groups better include salami, cheese, potato chips, and Diet Pepsi. She was using me as a visual aid to teach Chris what not to eat.

I walked across the road to the offices of the *Oakhurst Mountain Journal*, the weekly newspaper whose editor, David Ankney, had expressed concern over the arrival nearby (in mountain terms, forty miles is nearby) of the Eternal Truth Temple.

The young woman behind the counter just called out, "David! There's somebody here to see you," when I asked for Mr. Ankney. A moment later he appeared in a doorway to my right.

I introduced myself and in my still developing roundabout style told him my business without mentioning that I was actually working for the Temple.

Ankney asked to see my license and one other form of identification—a first for me. "You must be working for the Temple," Ankney said.

"Why do you say that?" I asked.

"Well, if you're working for them and you're a member of the Temple, you'd lie automatically. If you're working for them and not a member, you wouldn't want to announce it, because it is nothing to be proud of. And nobody else would be that interested in them to come up here to ask about them."

"You're right, of course. I'm working for the Temple. I'm looking for some missing property of theirs. I do not belong to the Temple. In fact, I do not belong to any organized religious group, or any unorganized religious group for that matter," I said.

"Preachers everywhere can rest easy, then," he joked. "I wrote a dandy editorial calling you a great American hero for that Carrick thing, but not many people outside central Oregon would have seen it."

"Can you tell me anything about the Eternal Truth Temple that might help me? Do they have any enemies?"

"Well, the Temple gives its membership at about a million, which probably means they really have about one or two hundred thousand. So that would pretty much leave the rest of the world's population on the enemy list."

"Come on."

"All right, I'm exaggerating. Most of the world either haven't heard of Yogi and Baba, and most of the rest don't care. You can put me with the 'don't care' group."

"You must care."

"I used to have a newspaper like this in Oregon a few years ago. Then I wrote some articles about a different Church, and strange things started to happen. Our well was contaminated, our pets were killed, my family threatened. One day I came to work and my newspaper didn't exist anymore. The building and all the equipment had burned to the ground." Ankney did not seem bitter and showed no emotion. He was merely stating the facts as if he were reporting the news. "So we moved down here."

"And then the Eternal Truth Temple shows up at your doorstep, so to speak."

"Yes. And after a brief, subtly worded editorial cautioning

against religious extremism, my car was stolen. It was later found at the bottom of one of our scenic valleys after a fall from the road above. Inside the wreckage were four crash dummies—one for each member of my family. The crash dummies were wearing our clothes."

"Say listen, Fisher, the Rajneesh toppled eventually. And I don't give these guys much of a shelf life either. So I'm going to concentrate on some easier targets for my pen, say the logging industry and the Department of the Interior."

I was disappointed I didn't do better, but there was no use annoying Ankney much further. "Thanks for your time," I said. "I wish you had something I could use."

"Are they paying you pretty well?" Ankney asked.

"What?"

"Are they paying you well?" he repeated. "The Temple, I mean."

"Yeah, pretty well," I admitted.

"Well, that's it then, isn't it?"

"What's it?"

"Money. The whole thing has got to do with money. Whatever is missing has to do with money. Where does the Temple get all their money? From selling those tacky little books at airports? Give me a break. It's got to come from somewhere else. We're not talking about Shakers or Shiites or monks here. These are people who are in this racket for the money. Also, their organization is crawling with ex-felons of every persuasion."

"Could be," I said.

"It's money," he said. "It's always money."

"Thanks again," I said, and left. They had one of those little bells on the door to let you know when someone comes in, or goes out.

Back across the street, Holly was waiting. Chris was awake now. "This was work, wasn't it?"

"Only a little," I said. "Let's hit the road."

The climb to Oakhurst had lowered the temperature about ten degrees. So it was only in the low nineties now. The higher we went, though, the cooler it got. At a certain elevation, sometimes called the "timberline," the trees changed. The oaks disappeared, replaced by sequoias. The trees were bigger, shading the roadway virtually every way it turned.

There were plenty of people in Yosemite Valley, as usual, but not so much as a holiday weekend. There was plenty of room to find a quiet spot near the Merced River, where we could look up and see where the falls had been reduced to a trickle because of the drought and lack of winter snow. The temperature was in the low eighties or high seventies, warm by most standards, but still more than twenty degrees cooler than the streets of San Joaquin. There was plenty of shade and a pleasant breeze.

If we lived closer to the coast, I would have suggested a ride to the ocean. Santa Cruz, or Morro Bay, or Pismo, or even Santa Theresa would be nice.

We thrashed around in the cold water until our legs were numb. The water level was low, but the current still strong enough to take little Chris all the way to Lake McClure if we didn't hold onto him.

"You know," Holly said. "I lived in San Joaquin all my life, and I had never been up here until I came with my Physical Geography class from City College." Holly went on for a while about exfoliating granite, glacial steps, flora and fauna all through the meal she brought. After we ate, Chris and I fell asleep under the trees. Holly read a book on economics.

She woke us up when she thought it was time to go. Darkness came early to the Yosemite Valley, and she dreaded the drive home in the dark. I volunteered to drive and, to my surprise, she let me. Chris fell asleep again before we reached the park gate. Holly fell asleep, too, while trying to read her economics book. I don't know how she does it.

Chapter 10

The morning after our Yosemite excursion, the air conditioning had been restored. Holly and her computer were busy earning most of our profits. I was sitting in my office with no idea about what to do next. Although I was getting paid for this activity, or lack of it, I felt I should be doing something, so I looked at the last of my folders from the Eternal Truth Temple's archives. I had already talked to Christy Black and Peter Rawson. Tommy Hammerhill was dead. The last one was Angie Fernandes.

Ms. Fernandes led an interesting life. Catholic girls school, now closed. Graduated from Lone Mountain College, which also no longer exists, since it was absorbed by the University of San Francisco. The woman was the kiss of death for her alma maters. Another interesting item in her resumè—she was a convicted felon, an ex-felon, technically, having paid her debt to society with supervised probation and "time served." Her crime, interestingly enough, was drug smuggling, albeit a small amount. Her drug rehabilitation was accomplished in the Temple's drug rehab program. More interesting was the fact that she managed to keep her position as an officer in a local Savings and Loan before, during, and after her "legal" problems and her affiliation with the Temple. No wonder there was a Savings and Loan crisis. Or, perhaps, it explained something for which I'd yet to find a question.

I took the Dart for a little cruise across town. There was no freeway to go east and west yet, although one was decades in the planning. There was an eight-lane-wide swatch of empty lots and abandoned buildings that looked like a tornado had ripped through town, but as yet, no pavement. I took Kings Canyon Avenue, which seemed to have an unsynchronized stop light every three feet, past the County Hospital, the Welfare Office, the Fairgrounds and billboards in Spanish.

This was "Sunnyside," so named, I suppose, because it was on the east side of the city where the rising sun first greets the city of San Joaquin. Sunnyside was one of those real estate agent descriptions used to associate their particular listing with the well-to-do, established neighborhood on Butler Avenue, similar to the one on Van Ness Avenue, rather than the distressed barrios that one passed through on the way there.

Sunnyside Savings and Loan sat in the southeast corner of a four-shopping-center intersection. I asked for Angie Fernandes and was pointed toward a row of desks by a smiling teller.

"Ms. Fernandes?" I asked, not depending on the name plate on her desk.

"Yes, may I help you?" she smiled.

She stopped smiling when I told her who I was, who I worked for, and mentioned the names Christy Black, Peter Rawson and Tommy Hammerhill. I sat down without being asked. She looked around furtively. "Couldn't this wait?" she fumed.

"I needed a calendar," I said.

"I don't know anything about the missing disc, Tommy Hammerhill or any drugs!" she answered quickly, quicker in fact than I had a chance to ask. I hadn't even mentioned drugs. But by telling me she didn't know, one could only assume she did know.

"Do you speak Spanish?" I asked.

"What?"

"*Se Habla Espanol*?" I repeated.

"The name is Fernandes. With an 'S.' That's a Portuguese name. I am not Mexican."

"That's not what I asked. Tommy Hammerhill wasn't a Mexican, and he spoke Spanish."

"I think you better leave," she told me, looking around for a security guard.

"Does this mean I don't get a calendar?"

On my way out I paused at a wall of photographs, individual shots of the Board of Directors of Sunnyside Savings and Loan. In the middle with the word "Chairman" under it was a picture of Mr. C. Thomas Baker.

Chapter 11

When I got back to the office, there was a message to call Cooper Page. He wanted to check up on my progress on the missing Sacred Disc, no doubt. Although I'd had an interesting last few days—I found a dead body, had been questioned by the police, had seen a naked rich woman, and fell asleep in Yosemite National Park—I couldn't honestly say that I had much information on the status of the missing sacred computer disc.

I didn't exactly want to say that to Cooper Page, though. So I skirted that particular subject and went fishing. "Cooper?" I asked. "Do you think there might be some drug connection with the missing disc?"

"No, I'm sure the Yogi and Baba—the Temple—has nothing to do with drugs of any kind," he answered quickly.

"I wasn't accusing them, of course, but there are hints of some connection, if not with the Temple, then maybe some members, or former members."

"What kind of hints?" he asked

"Well, Hammerhill's murder, for one. Christy Baker was shot full of drugs. Angie Fernandes is a convicted drug smuggler."

"Anything else?"

"Nothing specific, but the Temple collects a lot of cash. Cash that could be skimmed by Temple members for drug use. Cash that could be laundered from drug sources."

"What would any of this have to do with the missing sacred text?" Page asked.

"I haven't figured that out yet," I admitted.

"Well, stay on it," he said, "and keep abreast of whatever you're doing." He hung up without saying goodbye.

Holly brought some papers for me to sign, and wanted to show me the bank deposit she had finished. I signed the papers, but told her to take care of the bank stuff herself. Even if she was stealing from the company, I'm sure she was certainly smart enough to hide it from me.

I sat around the office for a while, until I developed a dual case of embarrassment and boredom. Boredom for not having anything real to do, and embarrassment because I had to sit there in the presence of Holly, the human dynamo, who probably got more work done accidentally than most people, particularly myself, did on purpose.

I picked up my files from the Temple and went upstairs. "I can't concentrate in here," I said to Holly.

Upstairs in my apartment I was able to concentrate. I read the sports pages and the comics and fell asleep on the couch.

When I was in Vietnam, and for some time after, I used to have this dream where men would come after me and try to kill me. I thought I was having that same dream again, when I realized they had never broken down my apartment door before. They had never spoken Spanish in the other dreams, only Vietnamese. And they had never punched me in the face before. They had never kicked me in the ribs with cowboy boots before.

This was no dream.

By the time I made the decision to fight back, I was pretty much incapable of it. I was knocked to the floor and then pinned there. I was kicked or hit—it really didn't make much difference—in the head, in the ribs, in the back, in the groin, and worse.

I had survived Vietnam, divorce, City League Basketball, but I was convinced I was going to die this time. I felt myself slipping into hell. God apparently was still tiffed over the Carrick incident. I heard screams and alarms. I saw flames.

The kicking and punching stopped, but not the screams, alarms and flames. The screams came from my attackers. The alarm was coming from their car outside. That's where the flames were coming from as well. Their car was on fire.

They left me doubled up on the floor. The car alarm eventually stopped, but was soon replaced by the more familiar sound of a fire engine siren. I lapsed in and out of consciousness. Every time I opened my eyes, something changed. Once I opened them and the siren stopped. Then the flames disappeared, though I could still see flashing red lights through the window. I opened my eyes again and saw Holly. I think she was crying for some reason. When I opened my eyes the next time I was in the back of an ambulance looking up at a paramedic.

The next time I opened my eyes I was lying in a hospital bed. A tube connected my arm to a plastic bag. The stuff in the plastic bag kept me from opening my eyes for long intervals. I looked up to see a very tall, very familiar doctor. It was my brother, the doctor.

My brother, the doctor, it was generally agreed, got most of the brains and height in the family. He had been six foot eight since the tenth grade. He was recruited by UCLA during their glory years. He went instead to Princeton, where he made all Ivy League honors, all while doing the pre med thing. He had his own priorities. I, of course, would have sold my soul for his ability and the chance to play for John Wooden.

He looked at my chart like he knew what it meant. His doctor face didn't betray his brotherly concern. "Your secretary, Holly, called me," he said.

"She's not my secretary."

"She still called me."

"So tell me, doctor, will I be able to play violin?"

"Sure, after years of lessons, practice and dedication. However, if you were still at Sierra Pacific, we would have to call this a season ending injury. Broken ribs, concussion, contusions. You'll be able to get around, but you're not game ready, and won't be for a while."

"I want a second opinion."

"O.K.," he said. "You're ugly, too." This banter was pretty much typical of our conversations for the last thirty years. "It's a good thing Holly is so sharp."

"What do you mean?"

"She pretty much saved your dumb ass. When she heard them beating you up, she broke the window of their Mercedes to set off the car alarm. Then she poured barbecue lighter fluid all over the leather upholstery and lit it."

"That explains the fire. I thought it was the gates of hell."

"Not surprising," he said. "She's in the hall."

"Holly?"

"No, Margaret Thatcher. Of course, Holly. What other 'she' would bother to come to see you?"

"You're right."

"I have to go watch the kid so she can come in."

He went out and Holly stepped in before the door had closed. She walked carefully and slowly toward the bed. She was smiling, but her smile looked as though it had been pasted on a sad face. Her eyes were red. It took me some time to realize she had been crying on my account.

"I've felt better," I said dumbly. "That tall doctor said I'd be all right. Funny, I can't help feeling I've met him somewhere before," I said, rolling my eyes.

It took her a moment to catch on, then finally her eyes smiled along with her mouth. "I didn't know who else to call," she said.

"There is no one else."

"He drove all the way from Stockton. He was here just a few hours after I called."

We had a moment of strained silence, then I said, "Thank you for saving my life."

"I'm sorry," she said for some reason. "I didn't know what to do. I had Chris with me. If I had a gun, I could have shot them or something."

"I think you did just fine."

"Well, I have to take Chris out of here and get back to the office."

"Yeah, I suppose one of us has to work."

"They say you can come home tomorrow. I told them to call me to come pick you up."

"O.K.," I said passively. "Holly?"

"Yes?"

"Thanks again, huh?"

"Sure." She left and my brother came back in.

"You're going home tomorrow. Do you need anything?"

"I doubt it. Holly has probably built a wheelchair ramp or an elevator to my apartment in her spare time."

"She seems fairly efficient. I have a dozen people working for me and any group of four or five of them could do her job."

"Yeah, I know," I said. "Would you mind if I gave her the Collection Agency and properties?"

"What do you mean?"

"In a will, you know, in case something happens to me."

"No, I don't mind. I'll manage to get by somehow."

"O.K."

"O.K. I've got to get back to Stockton. There are some real sick people waiting for me. Call me," he said. He always said "call me," but this time I think he really meant it.

"I will," I said, and I really meant it as well.

Chapter 12

Holly took me home from the hospital. My ribs and torso were wrapped tightly, my head bandaged. My swollen eyes were covered by sunglasses. It hurt too much to squint in the bright San Joaquin sunlight.

My apartment looked better when I got home than it had before the attack. Holly had not only cleaned up after the mayhem, but had done everything else that I had been ignoring. My coffee table was missing, however, having been broken beyond repair.

"What is this all about?" Holly asked me, watching Chris as he explored my apartment, careful that he not do any further damage to my place.

"I'm not sure," I said fairly honestly. "It might have something to do with this Temple thing, or with Christy Baker, but I don't know why or how. It could have been the same Mexicans that drugged Christy and killed Tom Hammerhill."

"I don't think they were Mexicans," Holly said.

"What?"

"Those guys," she said. "I don't think they were Mexicans."

"I heard them speak Spanish."

"Mexico isn't the only country in the world where Spanish is spoken, you know."

"What's the difference?"

"In English, you can identify whether someone comes from England, Australia, Boston, or Mississippi, can't you?"

"Sure."

"Well, it's the same in Spanish. Different dialects, different accents."

"Where are they from, then?" I asked.

"I'm no linguist, but it sounds like Central America or Venezuela, maybe Columbia."

"How do you know all this?"

"Spanish television. They have programs from all over Latin America."

The first visitors in my convalescence were Detectives Sanchez and Kaprelian. Sanchez immediately expressed his sympathy. "You look like shit, Fisher."

"Is it my hair?" I asked.

"What happened here anyway?" asked the reasonably efficient Kaprelian.

"I was asleep on the couch. Three men broke down the door and proceeded to kick the shit out of me."

"Could you describe them?" Kaprelian asked.

"Sure. They all looked like him," I said pointing at Sanchez, who didn't like the comparison.

"Three Mexican males, medium build," Kaprelian said, as he wrote.

"I don't think they were Mexican," I said.

"You said they looked like..."

"I know, but I didn't say they sounded like him. They had different accents, like they were from Central America, maybe Venezuela or Columbia."

"How do you know anything about that?" Sanchez asked incredulously.

"Spanish television," I said.

Sanchez rolled his eyes. Kaprelian corrected his notebook.

"Could I ask a question?"

"Sure," Kaprelian obliged.

"Did you guys hear about the Mercedes that got torched here the other night? Do you think that might possibly provide some sort of clue?"

Kaprelian flipped his notebook back a few pages. "It was reported stolen that same night."

"Before or after my assault?"

"Eight p.m."

"I was taped and tubed at the hospital by then," I said. "Who did the car belong to?"

They didn't say anything. They must not have heard me.

"Who did the car belong to?"

"It was registered to Eugenio Solis."

Solis was a well known name, often linked to racketeering, drug smuggling, immigration fraud, smuggling undocumented workers, that sort of thing. He'd been indicted, but never convicted of anything.

"Solis. Isn't he from El Salvador, or somewhere?"

"Honduras," spat Sanchez.

"Central America?"

"No, Honduras, Minnesota," Sanchez fumed as he walked out my new door.

Kaprelian closed his notebook and put his pen away. "We'll let you know if we get any suspects." He followed Sanchez out. I got up and locked my new deadbolts.

My first excursion to the outside world was to visit the law offices of Cooper Page. His office was downtown in a building full of lawyers. The county, state, and federal courthouses were all across the street, in a square called "Courthouse Park" for some reason. I insisted Page take a walk with me through the park.

"Is this good therapy for you?" he asked.

"No, it hurts like hell. I just didn't want to talk in your office," I said.

"Why's that?"

"Well, not long after our last conversation on the telephone, in which I merely hinted at the possibility of some kind of drug connection with the missing sacred disc, I was visited by the three *vaqueros* of the apocalypse."

"I hope you're not suggesting that I..."

"Wait a minute, I'm not done yet. Did I mention the burning Mercedes in front of my home and office?"

"No."

"Then I guess I didn't mention it was registered to one Eugenio Solis, a name frequently linked to the drug trade. Ever heard of him?"

"Sure."

"Of course, you've probably represented him."

"Don't I wish," fantasized Page. "He'd be a friggin' gold mine."

So much for the pursuit of justice.

"Is this all coincidence? I think not."

"So what are you saying?"

"All I am saying is that I think that maybe your phones or my phone could be tapped. I'd hate to think that my pain and suffering might be caused by some indiscretion on your part. If that were the case, I might..."

"Might what?"

I needed to work on some effective, yet snappy, all-purpose threats if I was going to remain an effective, yet snappy private investigator. I didn't have any on hand. "I'm not sure," I said.

"I'll have my phones checked," Page said. "Remember you can trust me. I'm on your side."

I wasn't convinced of either the "trust me" part or the "on your side" part. I'll bet Page's mother counts the silverware after little Cooper comes over for Thanksgiving dinner.

"Anything else?"

"Yeah." I pulled a handwritten piece of paper out of my pocket and handed it to Page. "I need a will drawn up. Just follow the instructions on that paper, make it all legal, you keep a copy and send me three copies. All right?"

"Sure," he said, looking at the paper. "You want to leave everything to your secretary."

"She's not my secretary," I corrected him. "Otherwise, yes."

"Sure thing," he said, smiling the wrong smile.

"And while you're at it, draw up a change of ownership. Make Holly Pena and I partners in Anderson Collections and Investigations. Fifty percent each."

"Whatever you say," he said. "Anything else?"

"Yeah, I'm back to work on the sacred disc thing. I'll deduct my 'days off.' And one more thing."

"Yes?"

"Don't send me a bill on this, either."

He laughed.

Chapter 13

I felt like hell for the next few days, sore and stiff, but I could get around and brain damage seemed moderate. I performed the few administrative tasks that Holly allowed me, but I had no idea at all about what to do about the missing sacred disc of my only client, the Eternal Truth Temple.

I was sitting downstairs in the office. Holly was picking Chris up at school, or taking him to soccer practice, when two strangely familiar men walked in. They were cut from the same mold—short, stocky Hispanic males wearing sports jackets and cowboy boots.

"Mr. Solis wants to see you," said the one on the right.

"Then tell him to come on in," I said.

"No, we're supposed to take you to him," said the same one.

"Well, I can't leave the office right now. Perhaps he could call and make an appointment."

"We're supposed to take you to him." The voice sounded the

same, but this time the lips of the one on the left moved.

They took a step toward me. I opened the top right drawer of the desk—it wasn't Holly's desk—and put my hand in the drawer and left it there. Their eyes widened and they didn't take anymore steps. With my left hand I took one of my cards off the top of the desk and held it out to them. "Here's my card. If Mr. Solis wants to see me, have him give me a call later and maybe we can work something out."

They didn't take the card, but left anyway. I supposed they could look the number up in the book.

When they were gone, I took my hand out of the drawer still holding the stapler it had been resting on. They didn't know how close they had come to me stapling them together.

An hour later, a phone call interrupted my reading of an interesting article in *Sports Illustrated* about the lack of defense in pro basketball. The call was from the office of Mr. Eugenio Solis. That's how they identified themselves, from the "office of Mr. Solis." I wondered what an actual person would sound like.

It seems the office of Mr. Solis wanted me to come and visit it. I told the office of Mr. Solis that I couldn't leave the office of Anderson Collections and Investigations at this time, but perhaps his office could come to my office. Then there was some hand over the mouthpiece before the office of Mr. Solis agreed.

Twenty minutes after the phone call, the two guys entered the office again. They left the door open this time and were soon followed by Eugenio Solis. He was about the height of his two bookends, but less beefy. He was a lot better dressed, no cowboy boots for him. All three of them didn't seem very happy to see me. Maybe it was the heat.

"Did you have an appointment?" I asked.

They looked even less happy. "Mr. Fisher, my name is Eugenio Solis."

"How do you do?" I said, and extended my right hand over the top of the desk. The heat had apparently fatigued Mr. Solis to such an extent that the three steps to shake my hand was too much for him. "I understand you are working for Mr. Baker," Solis said.

"You understand wrong," I corrected him. "Not that it's any of your business, but Mr. Baker did solicit my services but I had to turn him down, as I already had a client."

"Who would that be?" he asked.

"I can't tell you that one."

"Would it be the Eternal Truth Temple?"

"Like I said, I can't tell you."

"Well, if it was," Solis said, "it would be wise for you to drop that case and to avoid Mr. Baker as well. You see, one of my automobiles was recently stolen and set afire right outside your door. I believe you were the victim of a crime that night also." He didn't wait for a response, he just kept talking. "Despite my lack of knowledge and complete innocence in these matters, I do not wish to be connected with them in any way. Your government is currently engaging in a groundless vendetta against me, harassing my family, my legitimate business associates. These other matters, though unrelated to me in any way, only serve to give them another opportunity to make false accusations and create false evidence."

"Yeah, I've always hated the way my government mistreats foreign drug dealers. Isn't it a shame what they've done with that poor Manuel Noreiga?"

Solis' right bookend took a quick step toward me, then stopped and looked back at his boss. Solis neither spoke nor moved, which his employee must have taken as a sign to continue. He walked over to the desk which still separated us. "You've got a lot of nerve," he said.

I stood up. "You shouldn't talk about nerve with a tie like that." He looked down at his tie—its poorly tied knot led me to believe it wasn't a clip on—just as I grabbed it and jerked it down to the desk. His legs slipped out from under him and I had him sprawled face down on the desk. I kept choking him with my right hand pulling on his ugly tie. I picked up the stapler with my left hand and pummeled his face and head with it. Blood was coming out of his mouth and nose, not to mention the various cuts on his face and skull. I stopped hitting and choking him when he stopped thrashing around on Holly's desk. He wasn't dead. I could see his nostrils flaring, trying to breathe.

The whole thing must have only taken a few seconds because Solis and the other bookend hadn't moved. The standing bookend had his eyes widened, darting back and forth between his comrade on the desk and me. Solis had yet to change his facial expression or his stance. The bookend looked like he was going to make a move, so I reached into the jacket of the prostrate bookend and extracted a nine millimeter automatic. I pointed it up and snapped back the slide to put a round in the chamber. A bullet popped out when I did this, which meant there had already been one in the chamber. The bookend must have missed that part of the weapons safety course.

The combination of adrenaline and the gun in my hand gave me a tremendous feeling of power. The gun boosted my confidence level a few notches, too. "Get this piece of shit out of here, before you find yourself connected with another unpleasant police matter. And nothing else better happen around here or I'll make your fucking life so miserable, you'll be wishing for government harassment."

Solis didn't show as much fear as I would have liked, adrenaline, gun and all. Actually, he showed none. The standing bookend was nervous as he hefted his sleeping companion off the desk and out the door.

"Let me encourage you again to find another client, a client other than Mr. Baker or the Eternal Truth Temple."

"The job's not done," I said.

"If the Temple was to recover some missing item, would the job then be done?"

I thought for a moment. "You never know," I said. How did he know about the missing disc?

"Sometimes you will find that things have a way of turning up when you least expect it."

By the time I walked to the door, another big Mercedes was

pulling away. Only two heads were visible. Holly drove up just then with little Chris.

She looked at the gun in my hand but didn't say anything. She walked into the office before she said anything, and that was a loud "Sonofabitch!" It was my guess she had just seen her desk, now spattered with blood and a Bostich heavy-duty stapler similarly stained. She may have also noticed that all the items formerly on her desk were now on the floor.

I noticed Chris staring at the gun in my hand. I removed the clip and snapped back the action to remove the bullet in the chamber. I put the clip in one pocket and the gun in the other.

"Bob?" asked Chris.

"Yes, Chris."

"What are those policemen doing?"

"What policemen?"

"The ones across the street," Chris said, pointing to an unmarked police car with my old friends Sanchez and Kaprelian sitting in it.

"How did you know they were policemen?" I asked Chris.

"I don't know," he said. "They just look like cops."

"You're right, they do," I said. "Why don't you go inside and see if you can help your mother."

I walked across the street, around to the passenger seat where Sanchez was sitting. "Here's a hypothetical question," I mused. "Say they would have killed me, and then you actually arrested them, couldn't their lawyer get you for entrapment?" They were both sweating. I hoped it was from nervousness, but it was probably from sitting in a black car parked in the sun on a day when the temperature was 102 degrees.

"Do you have a permit for that pistol?" asked Sanchez, ever alert for any minor infraction of the law.

"Here," I said and tossed it on the seat between them. "I was just on my way to turn it in. It seems someone left it behind."

"Who was that?" Kaprelian asked.

"I think his name might have been Noreiga, because he got all upset when I mentioned Manuel's name." I dropped the clip in Sanchez's lap and left them sitting in the sun.

Back across the street, the office smelled like soap and ammonia. Holly's desk looked as good as new except for the stapler, which she was holding up for my inspection. "It's broken, but I thought you might like to keep it for a souvenir."

"Sure, why not?"

"That reminds me," she said. "We need to get some more barbecue fluid."

Chapter 14

I went upstairs to my apartment and put some ice on the hand I held the stapler with. It had swollen slightly and started to hurt more than slightly. The adrenaline that had coursed through my body with enough power for me to beat senseless with a stapler an armed hooligan had disappeared, gone to wherever it goes when it is not needed. I was tired. If I either smoked or drank, now would be the time to do one, or both, of these things. I went to the refrigerator and drank from the two liter Diet Pepsi bottle.

Maybe I was not cut out for this line of work. Old Anderson never had people breaking in and kicking his ass. I never recall him having to kick anyone's ass either. Maybe I was doing it wrong. My first assignment, the Case of the Missing Seventh Day Adventist, certainly hadn't prepared me for all of this.

Maybe I was too old. Maybe if I hadn't put Ben Carrick's eye out on national television, I could be back on a college campus somewhere, maybe even with tenure, lecturing glassy-eyed, disinterested undergraduates on the history of western civilization, and applying for a paid sabbatical to write some worthy historical tome that would only be read by other history professors. Maybe. Maybe the Sacramento Kings would play the Miami Heat for the NBA championship this year.

Why did Solis care about the Sacred Disc or the Eternal Truth Temple? Or Christy Baker? How did Tom Hammerhill fit in? The only thing they all had in common was money. And maybe drugs. Hell, most likely drugs.

There was a small knock at my door. It was little Chris. “Mom says you got a phone call,” he said. “Downstairs,” he explained further, just in case I was unclear on the concept.

I trudged down the stairs behind the little messenger. Once inside he pointed to the phone with the flashing red light just to be sure. I picked up the receiver and pressed the flashing red button. “Hello?”

“Mr. Fisher?”

“Yes.”

“This is Cecilia Baker. You remember, Christy’s mother.”

“Yes, of course.” How could I forget. “What can I do for you?”

“It’s all very distressing.”

Uh-oh, more distress from the Baker household. “What exactly is distressing?” I asked.

“Christy has run away.”

“Run away? Are you sure?”

“Well, she’s not here. Our lawyers told her not to go anywhere. We told her not to go anywhere. I didn’t know who else to call.”

"What about Mr. Baker?"

A cruel laugh was her only answer to that question. "Could you come by?"

"I don't know what I could do."

"Please," she said, in a voice which probably got what it asked for most of the time.

"Sure, I'll be right over."

"I'll be waiting for you, then," she said, and hung up.

I stood staring at the telephone in my hand. I finally hung up when I noticed Chris and Holly staring at me. "Well, I'm off," I said.

Chris said "bye" and Holly just smiled. I decided to take the Dasher, the economy car of our little motor pool. It wasn't new but had that sort of Volkswagen ageless quality. Besides, it at least came from the same country as Mercedes and BMW. I stopped at a 7-11 store and got a Big Gulp, rolled down the windows and made the trip north again.

I had pretty much finished the thirty-two ounces of Diet Pepsi just about the time all the ice melted. The gate to the Baker manse was open,so I drove in without asking the intercom. I hoped the Dasher wouldn't drip too much oil on the driveway. Volkswagens are notorious for leaking oil and the Baker's driveway looked cleaner than my kitchen floor.

As I approached the front doors they opened. Instead of Nash, the trusty butler, it was Mrs. Baker. Now I knew the reason for the double doors. It was so Mrs. Baker could make a dramatic impression on visitors like me when she opened the doors. She stood there smiling, back lit, standing on Italian marble, framed by a mansion. She was wearing a silk robe this time. Didn't the woman ever get dressed, I thought. That thought caused me to think of my last visit and what was, or wasn't, under the silk robe.

"Mr. Fisher." Her voice sounded relieved somehow. I didn't know why. If Christy was really gone, there wasn't a hell of a lot I could do about it now. "Christy's gone," she said. "I didn't know who else to call."

"Where's Mr. Baker?"

"Working or whatever."

"Does he know?"

"I left a message."

She closed the doors and I followed her to the solarium, where she picked up a glass and took a drink from it as we sat down.

"Can I get you something to drink?" she offered.

The thirty-two ounces of the Big Gulp hadn't worn off yet. "No, thanks," I said. "Have you called the police or your lawyers?"

"I beg your pardon?"

"About Christy. Have you called anyone?"

"No, just you. When I woke up she was gone."

"What time was that?"

"I don't know. About two."

"Did she take a suitcase? Any clothes?"

"I don't know. It's hard to say. She has a lot of clothes."

"Well maybe she just went out. She is an adult."

"Yes, but she is out on bail."

"That means she's not supposed to leave town, not her room."

"I'm just worried. You know, the bail and everything."

"Sure," I said. If Christy had skipped bail, then Mr. and Mrs. Baker would have to sell half of one of their cars to recoup the loss. "Perhaps one of the servants..."

"No, they're off today."

We sat silently while Mrs. Baker finished her drink. "Did you go to college?" she asked all of a sudden.

"Yes, I did."

"Is there a major for private detectives?"

"No, actually I was a college history professor before I became a detective."

"Really?"

"Yes." Perhaps I should carry around copies of my diplomas with me.

"I went to college for a while. That's where I met my husband." She got up and got herself another drink.

"What was your major?" I asked innocently.

"Drinking, dancing, and fucking," she said as she sat down next to me, followed by a hearty laugh. She drew one of her legs up on the couch, confirming my suspicions about what was under the robe. She didn't move her leg or cover herself.

"Didn't they do those things at your school?"

"Well, I got my bachelor's degree at Sierra Pacific, a school run by the Mennonite Brethren Church, who do not believe in drinking or dancing."

"What about fucking?" she asked, the robe coming apart.

"It's a small school. It wasn't offered as a major."

I think I'm as worldly as the next guy, so I took her conversation and near nudity as hints of seduction, but her hand rubbing my crotch pretty well convinced me. Suddenly our mouths were together, the robe disintegrated. Despite remaining joined at the lips, my clothes came off, clumsily, but quickly. Everything was happening quickly. In a short time we managed to perform acts still illegal, I think, in some states, not to mention the moral quandary of having sex with a married woman. I hesitate to call it making love, since love had nothing to do with it. It was over relatively quickly, the whole process accelerated by her desperate eagerness and, perhaps, my long absence from the world of sexual intercourse.

When adequate blood flow resumed in my brain, I felt stupid sitting there on the couch with no clothes on. What if Mr. Baker came home? Where was Nash, the trusted servant?

Still nude, Mrs. Baker made herself another drink. She was a very attractive woman. She was sexy. It had been a long time between sexual encounters for me. The part of me that didn't feel stupid, felt like going at it again.

"So, do you think you can find that little bitch before we lose the bail money?" Mrs. Baker asked.

Talk about a mood breaker. My desire for her waned suddenly and I got dressed. "I could try," I said. "Do you have any ideas where she might be, who she might call?"

"She has a psychiatrist, and she's in a couple of therapy groups, or support groups, whatever they're called. Other than that, who knows?"

"What's the doctor's name?"

"Furay," she said, exaggerating the pronunciation. "Foo-ray. He has an office on Herndon Avenue. Look for a white Jaguar in the parking lot. We paid for it."

Mrs. Baker was a petty, little egocentric bitch. Whoever said men often think with body parts other than their brains weren't far wrong in this case, especially just a few moments ago. If I were the sensitive type, I'd feel cheap and used about now. It's a good thing I'm not sensitive.

She was still naked. Her body had the power to excite. If only she could use that power for good instead of evil.

"If I find her I'll let you know," I said and left. As I was guiding the Dasher out of the driveway, I saw Nash, the butler, near the gate. He didn't look happy. I couldn't blame him. After all, he'd have to clean the oil spot the Dasher made on the driveway, not to mention the wet spots on the sofa.

Chapter 15

The third convenience store I stopped at had a public phone with a telephone book. I found Dr. 'Foo-ray's' number and called it. Using my rapidly developing detective lying techniques, I explained to a reticent receptionist that I was supposed to pick up Christy Baker after her therapy session but I wasn't sure what time it ended. Even though she said they didn't "normally give out that kind of information," I called to her attention Christy's recent legal difficulties with the law and expressed my concern that she, the receptionist, did not want to add to her, Christy's, problems and thereby incur the wrath of Mr. and/or Mrs. Baker. I was informed that the session would end at seven.

It was about five-thirty, so I decided not to brave the rush hour traffic all the way back to the Tower District. I went to Fatburgers and ate a double Fatburger with cheese, chili fries and a chocolate milkshake. It seemed the perfect meal to end a day of beating up foreign hoodlums and having sex with a married woman.

I stopped by another 7-11 store and got another Big Gulp Diet Pepsi and drove to the doctor's office. It was in one of the new medical building/office complex centers that have been popping up like weeds lately where fig orchards and grape vineyards used to be. There was still construction going on at this one. The contractor's trailers were still on site surrounded by temporary chain-link fences to protect the tools and equipment. Construction debris and odd lumber and bricks were piled up near newly landscaped lawn and shrubs which surrounded the freshly stuccoed and painted buildings like a green moat.

I sat in the car and listened to the radio. The Dasher only has an AM radio, and for some reason I can only get five stations—two Spanish stations, a country western station, and a news station from San Francisco. I also get a station from Boise, Idaho, but only at night. I could probably afford a new radio for the car, but these stations served me well enough. If I wanted to listen to something else, I could just take one of the other cars. The San Francisco station was broadcasting a Warrior's game. They were playing one of the expansion teams. There was a time when I seemed to know every player in the National Basketball Association. Now I can't name all the teams.

Finishing the Big Gulp, I suddenly had to urinate. I decided not to ask Dr. Furay's receptionist to use their restroom, so I left the Dasher and went to relieve myself behind the construction site. I chose a location between two huge dumpsters. After two Big Gulps and a visit to Fatburger, I was there quite a while.

Checking to see if my fly was zipped, I walked carefully across the construction mess. As I came around a pile of lumber I could see people coming out of the medical building. I quickly deduced they were Dr. Furay's therapy group. The deduction was made all the quicker since Christy Baker was among them. As I started over to her, I heard an oddly familiar click. There crouched in the shrubbery in front of me were two young men with red sweatshirts. It struck me as odd that anyone would wear a sweatshirt in this weather. It also struck me that it wasn't the best color to wear when hiding in the bushes for whatever reason. It then occurred to me that those particular sweatshirts were those favored by a certain Chicano youth gang. I assumed they were up to no good, an assumption pretty well confirmed when I saw what was making that familiar clicking sound. One of them held an M-16 assault rifle, similar to the one I carried in Vietnam.

I quietly started backing up. Beyond the bushes I saw Christy Baker separate from the rest of her group and walk through the parking lot toward the crouching red shirts. The one with the rifle raised it to his shoulder and pointed it in her general direction. I looked on the ground and found an adequate two by four. A few long strides, then the two by four came down hard on the shooter's head. There was a crunching sound. I'm still not sure if it was the boy's head or the lumber. Anyway, he dropped like a wet rag, his body over the weapon. I gave him another quick one to the back of his head and then turned to his partner. He had stood up completely by this time. His jaw dropped and his eyes widened which allowed him to better see the board coming toward his head. I caught him at the temple. It stunned him, his knees buck-

led, but he didn't go down. I wound up again and gave it another try on the other side of his head. This one laid him out over his comrade.

Christy ran up to where I was standing over the two youths with a two-by-four. "Fisher? What are you doing?"

I dropped the piece of wood, reached down and extricated the weapon from underneath the two "wannabe" gangsters.

"What's this all about?" she asked me.

"I don't really know, but they were pointing the gun at you.

"Who are they?"

"Got me. It's probably some sort of fraternity initiation ritual. Kill someone and get in the club."

"Why me?"

"Given your recent difficulties, I hardly think this is random. The name Solis springs to mind." I looked around. "I think we better go," I said.

"What about them?" she said, referring to the unconscious would-be assassins.

"Maybe they'll wake up and reconsider the direction of their young lives. Or maybe they'll run away out of fear of failing Mr. Solis. Or perhaps they'll lapse into a coma and die. I really don't care right now. Do you have a car?"

"No, I walked."

Still holding the M-16 by its combination suitcase handle and sight, I pointed towards the Dasher. In the back seat was an old gym bag with a pair of basketball shoes and some dirty shorts. I emptied the smelly stuff out, and disassembled the weapon.

There was a time when I had mastered the art of assembling and disassembling such a weapon blindfolded, a skill unpracticed of late. I put the parts in the gym bag and zipped it shut.

We drove west, my hands shaking on the wheel. I stopped at another 7-11 and bought another caffeine-laden Diet Pepsi. I'm sure I would be an alcoholic if so inclined. Instead I'm a cola-holic. It didn't help steady my nerves either.

"Why were you there, at Dr. Furay's?" Christy asked me.

"Your mother called me. She didn't know where you were."

"Don't tell me she was worried."

"Well, she was distressed, I can tell you that," I said.

"She's always distressed."

Both of us were quiet for a while, as I drove farther from the scene of the crime. The anxiety and adrenaline soon collided in my system and I began to shake like a leaf, a reaction to the caffeine and/or a reaction to violence.

"Are you all right?" she asked me.

"I'm a little shaken up, but it will go away after a while," I said, speaking from recent experience.

"Turn in here," she said, and I did without thinking too much about it or asking why.

We were driving on a narrow unpaved road through a fig orchard. She pointed to the left and I turned that way, onto another dirt road. When it came to an end, I stopped and turned off the car. On three sides of us were fig trees, fully leafed. Fig trees, the leaves and fruit especially, have a distinctive smell. Surrounded by an orchard of fig trees was a particularly pungent experience.

Such are the often overlooked pleasures of living in the nation's fruit basket. In front of us was the San Joaquin River, or the dry bed of the San Joaquin River. It was virtually dry now. Fifty years ago, about this time of year, salmon would be making their way upriver to spawn in the Sierra streams. The dam upriver put an end to that. There was usually a small token stream, but the recent drought had made the state less generous with "their" water. As dams proliferated on every river coming out of the Sierras, thirsty crops like cotton and rice appeared to suck up the water.

The quiet pastoral stream had pretty much calmed me down.

"When I was in high school, we used to come out here to party. You know, drink, smoke marijuana, have sex." She spoke without apparent remorse or guilt. "My father didn't know and my mother didn't give a damn. It was what she had done at my age and she didn't seem to care. I got tired of it all, though. That's how I got mixed up with the Temple. Those people seemed to care about me. The Yogi and the Baba were like perfect surrogate parents, or something. But they were full of shit, you know. They were no better than my parents, or drugs." Christy rambled on like this was our first date, and you had to summarize the last thirty years of your life, or in Christy's case, the last twenty, before dessert. "So now I'm in therapy," she continued. "Again," she sighed. "Even that is growing old. The longer I'm in it, the more I see it for as big a fake as the Temple was. I don't know what to do. I keep looking for something, but I can't manage to find it."

"Maybe you're not looking in the right places," I suggested, for lack of something intelligent to say.

"Like how?"

"You seem to be attracted to groups—parties, the Temple, the committee, group therapy. Then you're disappointed when the groups don't live up to your expectations. Just look to yourself, for a change. You seem to be a pretty decent person. I'm sure there's another pretty decent person out there waiting for you to find them."

"Like you," she said.

That's not what I had in mind.

"No, I meant someone your own age."

"Yes, I know. But still, it would have to be someone like you. I've only known you a few days, but already you've saved my life twice. I feel I can trust you more than anyone else in the world."

She kissed me, brotherly, gratefully. At first. But as the kisses continued, they evolved into something else. Kisses, caresses, fondling. I wished I had brought the Dodge. American cars, especially of that era, were at least subconsciously designed with what Christy and I were doing in mind. Not once while Christy and I were intertwined in the VW did I think about her mother and the events of earlier that afternoon. That would come later.

"Can we get something to eat?" she asked. "I'm starving."

"Sure. What would you like?"

"I don't care, just any place where they give a lot of good food."

"I know just the place," I said and pointed the Dasher toward the freeway. A few minutes on the southbound lane and I turned off on one of the downtown exits. There was a lot of bad feelings about the freeway when it was being built, but it sure shortened the trip downtown. We rattled around on streets which hadn't been resurfaced since the W.P.A. did them during the depression. On one side of the street were the Santa Fe tracks, on the other side were a row of large warehouses, some empty, some still in use. In the midst of this splendor stood our destination, the Woolgrowers Hotel.

"Have you ever been here?" I asked her.

"I didn't even know it existed."

I parked the car, and thought I might have made a mistake. Christy grew up with linen table clothes and silverware made of real silver. The Woolgrowers Hotel had neither of those. It was operated by a Basque family, and the "hotel" part was occupied primarily by Basque sheepherders when they weren't out tending sheep. Such hotels are common in the rural west where sheep are still raised.

There were three other Basque hotel/restaurants here in San Joaquin and I had been to others in Bakersfield, Reno and Elko. These places are known for good food at reasonable prices. The Woolgrowers is my personal favorite.

You have to walk through the bar and around a pool table and a shuffleboard table to get to the restaurant. The restaurant was crowded as usual, an eclectic crowd of downtown businessmen, local laborers and middle class families.

"Table for two?" I asked a swiftly moving waitress as she

passed by carrying two baskets of French bread.

"You can wait or you can find a spot at the boarder's table," she said without slowing down.

"Do you want to wait," I asked Christy, "or try the boarder's table?"

"What's that?"

I pointed to a long table lined on both sides by two rows of dark haired men passing large tureens of soup. "You eat with the boarders, the men who live here, the sheepherders."

"Sure, I don't care, as long as I get to eat soon."

We found two places across from each other. Christy Baker is a good looking woman, and her presence among a couple of dozen guys who spend months at a time alone with sheep didn't go unnoticed. If she was uncomfortable in these surroundings, she didn't show it. I wondered how Mr. and Mrs. Baker would like it here.

At the boarder's table there are no menus. Waitresses just start bringing food, lots of it. There were large baskets of French bread already on the table. We were passed tureens of thick vegetable soup without asking. You served yourself here, so we did. The sound of soup slurping came from both sides of the table. The ever-hustling waitresses didn't do much talking. When they thought you were ready, they brought more food. Next was a green salad, just iceberg lettuce with oil and vinegar dressing, again served in large bowls and passed around. In slightly smaller bowls were peas with some boiled potatoes and a sprinkling of carrots thrown in.

Christy seemed to be enjoying herself. The woman could really put away the food. Around us, some of the boarders were speaking Basque, a language unidentifiable if you didn't know what it was, with little apparent relationship to French or Spanish, the countries which surrounded the Basque homeland. The faces at this table were the faces of Picasso painted in Guernica.

The next course was a lamb stew with vegetables. The meat was so tender it almost melted in your mouth. Alongside were bowls piled high with a cold potato salad with tiny shrimp mixed in it. There were two main courses this evening—sometimes, there is only one, you never know until you get here—crispy fried chicken and lamb shanks, both on heavy platters passed around carefully. The chicken is a personal favorite of mine, but I couldn't resist the lamb either. It was sprinkled generously with chunks of garlic the size of chopped nuts on an ice cream sundae.

Christy was holding her own in total food consumption with the sheepherders, who nodded in appreciation at her agressive appetite and large pile of chicken bones. She drank red wine from a water glass poured from gallon jugs on the table. Dessert was the same for everyone, ice cream. Spumoni, tonight. I gave mine to Christy. I don't care for Spumoni.

When the bill came, she offered to pay for her half. I told her I could handle it. It was only seven dollars each.

"I've seen lamb, not half as good as this for thirty dollars at Ma Raison," she said, referring to a fancy northside eatery.

"That's why you'll never find me there," I said. "Do you

always eat like this?" I asked.

"No," she grinned, then blushed. "Just after, you know, good sex. Remember?"

"Oh yeah," I said, remembering.

Chapter 16

I drove back to my place. It was night, so I turned on the radio station from Boise, Idaho. A thousand miles away, in another time zone, another climate zone, playing music from twenty years ago. It seemed appropriate. Once back at my swinging bachelor digs, there was a more civilized, more relaxed reprise of the earlier scene in the VW, this time in a real bed.

This is where the comparisons begin. Christy supple, where her mother was taut. Christy soft, her mother sinewy. Christy sexually generous and giving, her mother, not.

In the morning I made breakfast. It seemed like the thing to do. I can actually cook. However, there doesn't seem much point in it for just myself. I made scrambled eggs, which came out pretty good. The bread in the refrigerator tasted better after it was toasted. Had I planned any of this ahead of time, I would have had bagels, or fruit, or hash browns, something to make an omelet. I would even have had coffee for her. I never drink it myself.

Christy was too polite to complain when I poured her a Diet Pepsi. I didn't have any milk, either. I cooked ten eggs. That was how many I had, and I cook better in volume. She ate most of them herself.

"There's something about multiple orgasms," she said, "that makes me really hungry." And I was hoping it was my cooking.

We made pleasant small talk, about food, growing up, San Joaquin, school, first date kind of stuff. I didn't inquire about the Temple, the sacred disc, drugs or dead boyfriends. I figured it would spoil the mood. There was no further discussion about sex. I also didn't mention my adventure with her mother.

She helped me clean up, and then I called her mother and told her that Christy would be coming home. Mrs. Baker thanked me, but I sensed a lack of genuine maternal concern.

"Thanks for calling for me," Christy said. "I can't stand to speak to her."

"That's all right."

"She's such a bitch, you know," Christy informed me.

I didn't say anything.

"Be careful," she warned me.

"Of your mother?"

"Her too," she smiled. "But I meant just be careful in general."

"Thanks. Are you sure you don't want a ride home? You could borrow one of the cars."

"No, I need to work up to it. I'll take the bus. It will take just long enough to get there."

I walked downstairs with her. She kissed me on the cheek and

I watched her walk away toward the bus stop. When she was out of sight, I turned to go back upstairs. Holly was watching me through the office window. She smiled. I went back upstairs and then I smiled as well.

I was still smiling when Lt. Sanchez appeared at my door. I know I was smiling because I consciously stopped when I saw him. I almost didn't recognize him without his trusty sidekick and faithful companion Kaprelian.

"May I come in?" he asked civilly.

Both the question and his manner caught me off guard. I was surprised he didn't just kick the door down. "What's up?" I asked.

"I was just in the neighborhood," he lied.

"Would you like a soda, or something? All I have is Diet Pepsi, though." I would have offered him something to eat, but Christy didn't leave much behind.

"No, thanks, I won't be here that long."

"Pleased as I am to see you, if you don't mind me asking, is this a business or a social call?"

"I guess you can call it a social call, since I am no longer working on the Hammerhill investigation."

"Why's that?"

"Who knows. That's just the way things work downtown."

"You know, Sanchez, I'm a little new at all this, so I don't know how things work downtown. Tell me, is this good news or bad news for you?"

"In the big picture, it doesn't matter much. As we speak, one of our fellow citizens is thinking about, planning, or actually killing another one of our fellow citizens, so I won't be idle for long. But it won't be as interesting as this one."

"Why's that?"

"The number of players. The average homicide we see just has two players, the murderer and the murderee. Is this too technical for you?"

"No, it's fascinating. Please continue."

"There's usually bystanders or relatives. But they're not usually very interesting. But here, you've got an attractive rich girl and a dead boyfriend in a shabby neighborhood, a religious cult, a foreign national suspected of drug smuggling, and a man who tried to kill a television evangelist on live television."

I let that one pass for the time being.

"No, it's not every day you get a group like that together for the same murder."

"So what happens to the case now?"

"Well, it can go one of two ways. The Baker kid has better lawyers than the city does, so there's a good chance she could walk if it goes to trial. If she walks, the cops blame the judicial system. If it doesn't come to trial, the cops are blamed for playing favorites because the accused is a rich white girl. Of course, it would be more interesting if the victim had a grieving family for the media to exploit or was a member of a minority in order to illicit a public outcry. I'm afraid little Tommy Hammerhill and this case will be long forgotten before the year's first raisins are dried." That meant late summer, early fall.

"At least these years on the job haven't made you cynical."

"What these years on the job have made me is aware of the big picture. In my time on the force, I've seen four different police chiefs and five different mayors. But I'm still here."

"So who's on the case now?" I asked.

"Wally Tuttle," Sanchez said without comment. None was necessary as even I knew Tuttle's reputation. He was a career ass-kisser of the highest order. And his nickname, "Wally the Turtle," came not only from his last name, but by his investigative style. He moved as slowly as a turtle, and only came out of his shell when it was safe.

"Well, I've got to go," Sanchez announced suddenly. "I'll let you get back to whatever it is that you do."

"Stop by any time," I said for some reason, and listened to him go down the stairs.

Chapter 17

On a whim, I grabbed a soda from the refrigerator and hopped in the Dasher. I got on the freeway and followed the familiar route to Yosemite. This time, however, I turned off about three quarters of the way and followed the road to the mountain home and headquarters of the Eternal Truth Temple. There were no signs to lead the way, but everyone knew where it was. There were only so many roads up here.

Eventually I came to a gate with a large Eternal Truth Temple sign above it. The gate was closed, but as I approached, a guard wearing camouflage fatigues stepped out of the gatehouse. He looked like a soldier, from his uniform to his crew cut, as well as the M-16 slung over his shoulder. It was the series of earrings in his right ear that distinguished him from the soldiers that I was used to.

I showed him my card and told him I wanted to see either the Yogi or the Baba, or both. No, I didn't have an appointment. He went back into the gatehouse and made a phone call. When he finally hung up, he opened the gate and pointed the way to where Baba and Yogi were.

The narrow ribbon of black asphalt led past a small group of utility buildings and a motor pool which included some tractors, vans, trucks, station wagons and four Rolls Royces. Beyond that was another set of buildings, prefabricated, modular boxes arranged in two rows connected by more black asphalt. Such buildings were a common sight on over-crowded California public school campuses, used as classrooms. Opposite those were another two rows of more traditional mobile home type buildings. The clotheslines, which led me to believe these were residences, were decorated with the white and orange robes of the faithful and the camouflage fatigues of those entrusted with guarding the faithful.

I shifted the VW into second gear for the gradual climb to the center of the Eternal Truth Temple's compound, and worldwide "empire." On the crest of a hill, sat a large pyramid. This was the main temple of the Eternal Truth Temple. I'm sure the pharaohs of ancient Egypt would have erected something similar had steel framing, glass and concrete been the favored construction techniques of their day. The pyramid could supposedly hold 7500 of the faithful, in air conditioned comfort—you could see the ducts through the glass. Surrounding the big pyramid were three smaller versions, one of which, the chamber of the Baba and Yogi, was my destination. The others I assumed were the offices of the vast Eternal Truth Temple's spiritual and business empire. The pyramids were connected by a series of variously colored concrete pathways and semiarid landscaping, suited for the lack of water as well as the desert motif suggested by the pyramids—palm trees, buffalo grass, mesquite shrubs.

There was no parking lot, so I just pulled the Dasher off to the shoulder and parked it. I left the windows open and the door unlocked. I knew it would still be hot when I left and I was hoping there wouldn't be any car thieves in such a holy place. I followed the gold path to the pyramid where the guard told me I would find the Baba and Yogi. I felt like Dorothy following the yellow brick road to the Land of Oz. It was a little different. In this scenario, to see the great and powerful wizards, I had to pass through a metal detector and sit in a waiting room. The Eternal Truth Temple and my dentist bought their furniture at the same place.

"The Baba and the Yogi will see you now," an orange robed woman announced, and led me to a large room with no furniture, except for two chairs on a raised platform at the far end of the room. The Baba and Yogi were sitting in the chairs. It looked like a throne room in a movie or a play. The Baba and Yogi were still in costume—Baba in the Nehru jacket and the Yogi in his white robe. This hall, I figured, was a mini-version of the larger pyramid where more intimate groups of the faithful could listen to the masters and do whatever it was that these faithful did. Whatever it was, they did it without any chairs.

"Mr. Fisher," the Baba spoke, "what a pleasant surprise. Have you some news for us concerning the sacred disc?"

"I believe it will be returned very soon," I said, although I had no real indication that it would ever be returned, or even where the thing was. "The purpose of my visit is to ask you whether you know of any temple members, past or present, with an involvement in drugs."

"Drugs?" The Yogi seemed astonished.

"Yes. Tom Hammerhill's death was drug related, and Mr. Solis, a man with drug connections, seems suddenly concerned with my activities."

"As you may know," the Baba said, "the Temple provides an extensive drug rehabilitation program. So while many of our followers may have had a history of drug abuse, we have eliminated that evil from their lives."

"Could there be a chance of missing someone, here or there? Let's face it, you have a large, world-wide organization through which much money flows. Could it be possible..."

The Baba interrupted me. "All monies are closely guarded and all activities of our people well accounted for."

"So you see," the Yogi added, "what you are proposing is simply not possible. We do, however, appreciate your professional concern and note it well."

Now it was the Baba's turn again. "But there is no connection, whatsoever, with drugs, the Temple or the missing sacred disc."

"And Mr. Solis?"

"We know nothing of him."

"And now," the Baba announced, "you must excuse us. It is time for our daily meditations."

"Of course," I said, not wanting to interfere with spiritual activities. As I was leaving the pyramid, I faintly heard the theme music to "All My Children."

The drive back to the valley was hot, the temperature rising as the elevation decreased. At the nearest mountain store/gas station/bait shop I bought some gas and a six pack of Diet Coke. I drank four of them by the time I got back to the office.

Back in my apartment, I took a shower and went downstairs to the office.

"You had a phone call from Cooper Page this morning," Holly said. "I told him you were indisposed."

"You should have rang me upstairs."

I dialed his number and only had to talk to a receptionist and a secretary before Page himself came on the line. "Good work, Bob. The Sacred Disc has been returned."

"I had a feeling it might be," I lied.

"The Yogi and the Baba are very pleased," he said.

"Well, I did my best," I said modestly.

"Of course you did. And they have authorized me to give you a bonus in addition to your regular fee. The check will be in the mail this afternoon."

"I appreciate that, Cooper," I said. "Just one more thing?"

"Yes?"

"Do you know who returned the disc?"

"No, it just showed up in the mail. Good work, Bob. We'll be seeing you."

After he hung up, I got a Diet Pepsi out of the office refrigerator. Every time I talked to him, it made me want to rinse my mouth out.

Holly was staring at me.

"Was there something else?" I asked her.

She hesitated and then spoke. "Mr. Page's office also wanted something else."

"Like what?"

"They wanted some personal information about me—full name, address, social security number—something about a partnership agreement and a will," she said, turning the last part of her sentence into a question.

"Oh, yeah, I meant to tell you about that. You're becoming a partner. You'll get fifty percent of the business and the property."

"You're not serious."

"You generate most of the revenue, do eighty percent of the work, so it's only fair that you get fifty percent of the business and profits."

"Mr. Fisher."

"Since we're partners, you can't call me Mr. Fisher anymore. You'll have to call me Bob."

"But..."

"But nothing. It's not like I built this place up from the ground. It just sort of fell into my lap. You've been here longer than I have and know more about it. So, from now on, I'll be the investigations half and you'll be the collections half."

"Then I can make decisions, do whatever I think is right?"

"Isn't that pretty much what you've been doing for a while?"

"Oh, I've got lots of ideas. I think we could make some real money around here. I was thinking we could add a credit bureau to run credit checks and histories and..."

She did have some ideas. However, I interrupted her. "Do whatever you think is right. Hire some employees, give us whatever salary you think we can afford."

"This is great. Thank you. You won't be disappointed. I won't let you down."

"Don't go all gushy on me. Try not to land us in bankruptcy court, or any other court, and we'll be all right. And stop paying the rent on your apartment. You own the building now." She smiled at that one perk that might have escaped her mind. "Do you need anything from the store? We're almost out of soda."

"No, I'm fine."

I started for the door, but she stopped me. "Bob," she said tentatively.

"Yes?"

"About the will?"

"What about it? If I get hit by a bus on the way to the store, you get everything."

"But why me?"

"Who else? My brother, the doctor, has a car that costs more than this building," I exaggerated, but only slightly. "Anderson should have left you a piece of it in the first place," I said. "By the way, do you think we should change the name? There is, after all, no Anderson at Anderson Collections and Investigations."

"We better not. The name is well established and, let's face it,

I'm an unwed Mexican mother, and you have a reputation that... you know."

"I know."

"Anderson has a solid Nordic ring to it," she said. "Besides, we've got all this stationery."

"Whatever. It was just an idea."

"What we could do is create a subsidiary. Use a Spanish name. Target the Hispanic community. That's a whole new market for us."

"Slow down, I don't even have my Porsche picked out yet."

I headed for the store, fully expecting to be on the New York Stock Exchange and a millionaire by the time I got back.

Chapter 18

I decided to walk to the store. A cooling trend had dropped the temperature to the high 80s, low 90s. I skipped the sidewalk and chose to walk along the canal. I climbed up the levee and headed north as the swiftly moving water traveled south. The water, I knew, was cold without having to touch it. It was recently snow in the Sierras, now on its way to irrigate the field of the nation's leading agricultural county.

Originally there had been a natural creek here, called, even by the Indians, "Dry Creek." The name hinted at its usual water level. When the farmers, water companies and state created the valley's irrigation systems, they often followed existing rivers, creeks, and washes. This part of the canal is still called the "Dry Creek Canal." This time of year it gave the houses that border it a riverside atmosphere, and the air seems cooler near it. The rest of the year it was an empty, miles long pit, littered with trash, old tires, and abandoned shopping carts.

Canals like this one used to criss cross the city in every neighborhood, a reminder of the city's economic base—agriculture. Even as the city grew into formerly rural and farm areas, the canals remained. But this is no Venice. Not the one in Italy. Not the one in Southern California. The canals were built to bring water from the mountains to the fields. Boating was not permitted. Nor was swimming, though many have done it, and continue to escape the summer heat with a jump off a bridge.

And every year the news includes more than one story about a person, adults occasionally, but more often children, found dead in one of the canals. While the water may be inviting, it is also deceptive. The current, at peak season, is swift and unyielding. The water, despite the air temperature outside, is numbingly cold. The sides of the canals are steep, often made of concrete with no easy way to climb out of the fast-moving water on one's own once you're in. Every so often the canal itself disappears altogether, as the water goes into an extensive system of huge pipes. Recently, as public outcry has increased with the tragedy of yet another lost child, the canals have been rechanneled into subterranean aqueducts, their former watery paths converted to bike and jogging paths or commercial use. That is what had happened to sections on both ends of this canal. But this stretch remained through this often anachronistic neighborhood, which looks much as it did thirty or forty years ago, except for an occasional backyard satellite dish and the recycling bins on trash pick-up days.

I walked around the first of three bridges that punctuated the relatively short walk. Under each bridge is a steel grate to catch the flotsam and litter. I looked back as I walked, but then stopped. Out of the water, churning around tree branches and through the grating, an arm was sticking out of the water, stiffly frozen as if still reaching for a way out of the canal. Painted fingernails, a woman then, but then you couldn't always be sure in this neighborhood. Black hair swirled among tree leaves, floating beer cans and styrofoam cups.

I ran the rest of the way to the store, called 911 on a pay phone. I described the situation and gave the location. I jogged back to the bridge and was there when the police and paramedics arrived.

The first police officers blocked off the area with that yellow tape. A small crowd had gathered to watch the paramedics fail to extricate the body from the water. The deceased was apparently stuck on something beneath the water level, probably the same steel grating that stopped her at this spot. A call was made, and while we all waited for the sheriff's diving team to respond, Sanchez and Kaprelian arrived.

"When I said we wouldn't be idle for long," Sanchez said to me, "I didn't expect you to go out and find something for us to do."

"I'm afraid I'm just one of those uninteresting bystanders this time."

Kaprelian took my statement again as Sanchez walked around the canal and bridge. A sheriff's van arrived and two men in wet suits and oxygen tanks emerged and waddled to the water's edge, attached a line to themselves and eased into the water. They soon dislodged the body. The victim was pulled from the murky water by the paramedics.

The body was stiff, the one arm still frozen, still reaching up. Her long hair was tangled with debris from the canal. She was wearing a jogging suit with one jogging shoe. The other foot was bare.

The crowd, now larger, groaned at the sight, but did not turn away as the paramedics searched the pockets, but found nothing. They placed the body in the familiar black body bag.

Sanchez and Kaprelian took a look at the body before it was zipped up, then looked at each other. Kaprelian looked for me, and motioned me over to where they were.

"Do you know her, by any chance?" Sanchez asked. "You do live in the neighborhood." I realized this meant they wanted me to look at the body. I hesitated, but when Kaprelian held up the cover, I took a quick look, then turned away. A quick look was all it took. "Her name is Angie Fernandes."

"You know her?" Kaprelian seemed surprised.

"Not really," I said. "She works at a bank I went to recently. Sunnyside Savings and Loan."

As Kaprelian wrote that in his notebook, Lt. Wally Tuttle appeared. It was over an hour and a half since I had called 911. Tuttle was a chubby little guy for a cop, I thought. His eyes, just above his chubby little cheeks, were mere slits, as though he was perpetually squinting into the San Joaquin sun, even though we were well in the shade of the trees which lines this part of the canal.

"This becoming a hobby with you, or something, Fisher?" Tuttle asked me. "Finding bodies, I mean."

I didn't answer him, waiting instead to see if he had anything worthwhile to say.

He didn't.

"The coroner should just follow you around," he joked, though no one laughed, much less imitated his stupid little smile. "At least this one is accidental," he said. Sanchez and Kaprelian shot each other a practiced glance that spoke volumes. "She was probably jogging and fell into the canal," Tuttle surmised. "It happens all the time."

I finally spoke. "Yeah, she drove all the way across town to jog along this glorious three block stretch of canal bank where she would have to climb over a concrete bridge every block."

Ever the philosopher, Tuttle observed, "Stranger things have happened."

Like him being a police detective.

"Or maybe it was suicide. What do you think, guys?" he asked Sanchez and Kaprelian.

"Hard to say," Kaprelian said, speaking for the both of them, as they both shrugged their shoulders, in the universal gesture known to all soldiers, civil servants and people in general who are in a subservient position to idiots like Tuttle.

Satisfied, Tuttle walked over to his car and drove away to solve the next crime. "So what happens now?" I asked.

"Do you flip a coin—heads for suicide, tails for jogging accident?"

"What we do," Kaprelian explained, "is wait a day or two for the medical examiner to identify those cuts and bruises on her face to be caused by a beating, not a fall into a canal. So the truth eventually emerges, and we don't have to personally make Tuttle look like the fool he really is."

"The 'big picture,' eh Sanchez," I said.

"Speaking of which, you know something else about her, don't you?" Sanchez asked.

The sacred disc had been returned, and this was the second dead body I'd seen in the last few days, not to mention the near miss on Christy Baker or me, so I decided to forget anymore of that client confidentiality bullshit. "She was a former member of the Eternal Truth Temple. She knew Tom Hammerhill."

The two policemen looked at each other again. Longtime married couples and police partners seem to have this non-verbal communication thing down to a science. "Anything else?" Kaprelian asked.

"Yeah, it's Fernandes with an 'S.' It's Portuguese, not Spanish."

He corrected his notebook. I continued my errand to the store. I bought a cold two-liter bottle of caffeine-free Diet Pepsi, as if I would be able to sleep tonight.

Chapter 19

I didn't sleep and I was headed east in the Dasher when the sun started coming up in my face. I drove back to the Sunnyside area to the late Angie Fernandes residence. It was a nice apartment complex, beautifully landscaped with a small concrete lake with a little concrete waterfall which recycled the same water over and over. Her apartment was on the ground floor and despite the expensive landscaping, the builder cut a few corners on security. I lifted one of her sliding glass doors off its track and stepped into her living room.

I looked around a little before I started getting nervous. Breaking and entering. Tampering with evidence. I'm sure the police might drop by some time soon. The thought of a potential roommate or spouse didn't occur to me until I'd seen the single bedroom.

The apartment was decorated in a minimalist Yuppie style. Single Henredon sofa, no coffee table, single floor lamp, state of the art compact disc player, microwave and Cuisinart. The refrigerator held three kinds of bottled water, four kinds of mustard and at least six different flavored vinegars. On the counter a wine rack and answering machine. An answering machine with a blinking light. Two blinks for two messages.

I found the 'play' switch and pressed it with a paper towel. The message was in what I supposed was Spanish, though I'm not sure what Portuguese sounds like. Even in a foreign tongue on an answering machine tape, the whiny voice of Peter Rawson was unmistakable. There was the sound of cars and noisy children in the background, so he was probably calling from a pay phone. The next voice was also both familiar and unmistakable. It was the resonant voice of the Baba Der Ursus.

Still using the paper towel, I popped the tape out of the machine, put it in my pocket, and stepped back outside through the glass door, replacing the door back on its track. I took another look at the lake and waterfall. Maybe I should get up this early every day. Right now was as cool as the temperature was going to be all day.

No one seemed to be awake yet in the complex, but as I pulled away in the Dasher I began to see signs of life—a paper girl on her bike, joggers in day glo spandex.

A 7-11 store was not far away, and I found it bustling with activity, doing a brisk business in coffee, newspapers and cigarettes. I stood before the soda machine, confronted with that paradox that has stopped me in my tracks many times before—if the 32-ounce Big Gulp costs eighty-nine cents, how can the 44-ounce

Super Big Gulp cost sixty-nine cents? Harjinder, the clerk, in his red vest covered with the 7-11 logo and a coral turban didn't know either. Perhaps that was the way it was done in the Punjab, where he was from.

When I returned to home and office it was just coming up to six a.m. and Holly still hadn't opened the office. Some partner. I went upstairs to my apartment and turned on the early morning news. The newscaster mentioned last night's unfortunate drowning in a local canal, but did not mention any names or advance the unpopular theories of Sanchez and Kaprelian. It took the weather person five minutes to explain that it was going to be hot in the valley, cool in the mountains, and cooler still at the coast. It was during that presentation that I fell asleep.

I awoke with a jerk to find a soap opera on television. It seemed there were illegal, immoral, unethical, and illogical things going on in some small fictional American city. That's why I don't like soap operas. They're not realistic at all.

Chapter 20

It was around eleven o'clock and Holly had finally opened the office. "Hi!" Chris greeted me cheerily from the floor where he was surrounded by computer paper, crayons and books.

"Good morning everybody," I said. I handed Holly the cassette. "Could you translate this?"

She held it up to her ear and shook it. "I can barely hear it," she smiled.

"Don't we have a tape player somewhere?"

"Sure. Chris, bring Mommy your tape player." Chris began an intensive search for his tape player, under chairs and tables before finding it under the old computer paper on which he was coloring. His smile said he was pleased with his discovery, happy to be of help.

It was a child's tape player, brightly colored with large buttons. Holly inserted the tape and pressed the large "play" button. We were all startled when it began. Chris had apparently turned the volume knob to its maximum. Holly turned it down and started it again. The voice of Peter Rawson filled the room, this time at a more reasonable decibel level.

"This is a white guy, isn't it?" she said, more than asked.

"Yeah, how did you know?"

Holly gave me one of those knowing looks so popular with mothers, teachers, wives, etc.

She listened, then turned it off. "He's warning her. 'Don't trust anyone,' he says. He says they should get out of the country."

"Anything else?"

"He wants her to call him when she gets home."

"Well, that's not going to happen."

"Why?"

"She was the one they pulled out of the canal last night."

"Oh, Jesus."

"There's another message," I said. Holly pressed the button again and we were in the room with the voice of the Baba Der Ursus, also in Spanish.

"He wants to meet her—tonight, the message says, so that must mean last night. He says it is very important. He will meet her at the Saigon Cafe, you know the one, it's over by..."

"Yeah," I said. I knew where it was. It was only a few blocks from here. The Dry Creek Canal runs right next to it.

"Why do you think they spoke Spanish?" I asked.

"What?"

"Why speak Spanish, these aren't native speakers, after all."

"I don't know. Maybe the same reasons we Chicanos sometimes speak Spanish when we can just as easily speak English."

"Why?"

"So the *gabachos* around us can't understand us."

I left the cassette with Holly with instructions to call Lt. Sanchez and have him come and get it. I told her I had an errand to run and took off in the Dasher, heading north toward San Joaquin State. I found a parking space in Little Saigon, nee Sin City. I got out of the car and took my gym bag with me. It was a little under ten pounds heavier than usual as it still contained the disassembled M-16 I liberated the other night from outside Christy Baker's psychiatrist.

I knocked on Peter Rawson's door. He tried to slam the door in my face when he opened it and saw me, but I was quicker and stronger. I pushed it so hard it sent him reeling backward, almost tripping over his laundry arrangement on the floor.

"Whadda you want?" he inquired impatiently, rubbing the spot where the door hit him on the head.

"This is a condolence call."

"A condolence call. I've come to pay my respects as per the recent loss of your loved one."

"What are you talking about?"

"Angie Fernandes."

"What about her?"

"Jeez, you are slow. They fished her body out of the Dry Creek Canal last night."

Rawson stopped rubbing his head, the pain replaced by one

more severe somewhere else inside of him. "How?" was all he could manage.

"Well, that's up for debate," I explained. "Lt. Tuttle is fairly sure it's a jogging accident. However, there are two other detectives who think she may have been beaten up before she hit the water."

He didn't say anything.

"So where were you two planning to go? And with what money?" He looked surprised. "I heard the tape," I said, by way of explanation.

"But..."

"I know. It was in Spanish. No, I don't speak Spanish, but let's face it, this is San Joaquin, California. It didn't take long to find someone who does."

"You better get out of here," he fumed.

"That's the proper attitude," I said, setting the gym bag down on the floor and kneeling down beside it.

"I mean it. Get out of here, or I'll..."

"You'll what?" I unzipped the bag and removed the pieces of the M-16.

"I have connections. I know people. I could have you killed."

"If you're talking about Solis, they've already tried twice and failed. And if you're talking about the Baba, his voice was on the tape right after yours. He wanted to meet Angie down by the Dry Creek Canal. I suppose it's only coincidence, that that's where she died." He shut up and went blank at that one. "Now a few years ago, I could put one of these together blindfolded in less than thirty seconds. I'm a little rusty, but I can still do it. Unless you tell me everything you know about all this, I'm going to kill you as soon as I get it assembled."

"You wouldn't," he said incredulously.

"Why not? When I was about your age I killed people for three hundred and fifty six dollars a month. One more on my conscience won't make much difference one way or the other."

"What do you want to know? I don't know anything. Honest."

"For some reason I don't think honesty is one of your finer qualities. If you don't know anything, then let's start with who you know. You knew Angie Fernandes. She had a drug problem, she worked at a bank. She was a member of the Temple and the Committee against the Temple. You knew Tom Hammerhill. Dead also. Also a former member of the Temple and Committee. You know Christy Baker, former drug user, Temple and Committee member, now up for murder. You also know the Yogi and the Baba, holy men and spiritual leader to millions—thousands, anyway. And you know Mr. Solis, Latin American drug kingpin."

I was just about finished with the weapon. I stood up and put the clip in my back pocket. I pointed the weapon at Rawson for effect. "Kneel down on the floor," I commanded. "A round from this thing could pass through you and still go through the wall. I wouldn't want any innocent people to get hurt."

He fell to his knees, not necessarily to protect his neighbors, but to beg. "Please don't kill me. I'll tell you whatever you want to know."

I still had the unloaded gun pointed at him. "O.K., let's start with Rosario Solis and the Temple."

"The Baba and the Yogi and Rosario grew up together. They were old friends."

"How did they grow up together?"

"In the Panama Canal Zone. Rosario's father was a worker there. The Baba's dad worked as an engineer on the canal and the Yogi's father was stationed there in the service. They were in sort of a gang—*Los Osos*."

The Bears. Even I knew that much Spanish.

"After the Baba and Yogi started the Temple they got together with Solis and went into the drug business. They used the Temple's network to smuggle and move the stuff. They used the Temple's finances and Angie's bank connections to hide the money."

"Most of the people that work for the Temple were recruited for some skill. That's why you see a lot of ex-cons and junkies. They bring a particular field of expertise to the organization drug sales, chemistry, murder."

"Where do you fit in?"

"I'm good at two things, drugs and computers. I made a program that organized the whole drug operation while hiding it in the regular Temple operation." He smiled as though he was proud of this accomplishment.

I waved the M-16 around a little and he stopped smiling.

"What about Tom Hammerhill and Christy Baker? What did they have to do with the drugs?"

"Nothing. When they were with the Temple, they were believers. Most of the believers don't have any knowledge of the drug system."

"What about the Committee against the Temple?"

"That was a legitimate thing. Angie and I were told to join it by the Yogi and Baba to keep an eye on Tommy and the Committee, and, I think to distance Angie and myself from the Temple if the drug thing was ever discovered. I think they planned for us to assume any blame if it ever came out."

"Was it discovered? Is that why Hammerhill was killed and why someone tried to kill Christy?"

"Not exactly discovered, but compromised."

"What do you mean?"

"Tom got his hands on one of the computer discs."

"The Sacred Disc?"

Rawson grinned. "The Sacred Disc is a joke. There are hundreds of Sacred Discs. They're like pieces of the cross. The Baba and Yogi pass them out to the rich believers and tell them not to tell anyone else. Of course, the believer then turns over all of their assets for such an honor and a privilege."

"Then what did Tom Hammerhill have?"

"He had one of the Sacred Discs with the drug program on it. The program was hidden in the disc. He couldn't find the way in. He couldn't break my code."

"He was talking to someone about computers the day he died."

"That was me. He wanted me to try it. That's funny, isn't it? I wrote the program and hid it, and then he wants me to find it."

I didn't share Rawson's sense of humor. "Yeah, that's really funny. I bet if he were alive, you two would be having a big laugh about it right now." He lost his grin again. "Where's the disc now?"

"I've got it. He gave it to me before he was killed."

"Get it for me."

I watched him walk over to the kitchen and reach behind the refrigerator. It didn't occur to me at the time that he could be reaching for a gun. I hadn't even loaded the M-16 yet. All he brought out, however, was a flat computer disc in a plastic bag.

"It's pretty much obsolete now," he said. "The Temple is changing computer systems."

"What were you going to do with it?"

"Angie and I were going to use it to squeeze some money out of the Temple, then go to South America, Brazil," he said. "Angie and I..." He got a far away look in his eye and didn't finish the sentence.

Rawson was a scrawny, greasy little weasel. Angie Fernandes was an attractive, well scrubbed, well-educated woman. How the two of them ever got together is beyond me.

"Where does Christy Baker's father fit in all this?" I was fishing.

Rawson's far away look was replaced by his surprised look. "He doesn't really, but the Yogi and Baba think he does. They were using Sunnyside S & L through Angie long before Baker joined the Board of Directors. Then when the disc disappeared they assumed it wouldn't be long before Tommy cracked the code, then Tommy tells Christy, Christy tells Daddy, Daddy calls the Feds. Then when you helped Christy and talked to her father, they thought that was too much of a coincidence and thought that you must have something on them."

I took the disc and put it in my shirt. "Come on, we're going to the police." He didn't seem to like that idea by the expression on his face. "They've already killed Hammerhill and Angie. What do you think they're going to do with you?"

I believe he understood the dilemma. He was screwed one way or the other. At least the police wouldn't throw him in a canal.

He was putting on his shoes when the door burst open. I saw the gun in the man's hand and acted instinctively. I swung the rifle butt across his face. As he was reeling and before he hit the floor, I administered another quick blow straight to his face again. This one shattered his jaw and pretty much ruined his nose. He was just hitting the floor when I turned to face an automatic directly in my face. I recognized the type of weapon. I recognized the ugly tie. I recognized the bruised and bandaged face of the Solis thug whom I last saw being carried out of my office. In my present predicament, an unloaded M-16 was as useless as a Bostich stapler.

I was relieved of the rifle and Rawson and I were ushered outside by three gun-wielding Hispanic males. Another of the group carried out their fallen comrade. Outside, the neighborhood was oddly deserted, except for two long black limos parked on the street. Rawson and I were pushed towards one while the bleeding hoodlum was taken to the other.

Inside the limo, we were greeted by the Baba Der Ursus and Solis. The limo was spacious and opulent, VCR, TV, liquor cabinet, telephones. Unfortunately, I couldn't enjoy it in comfort as I was sitting on the M-16 clip, still in my back pocket. I also had the computer disc in my shirt and a nine millimeter automatic pistol pressed against my throat.

"Nice car," I said. "What kind of mileage do you get?" I guessed no one ever stopped to figure it out because I didn't get an answer.

"I didn't tell him anything," Rawson nervously interjected. "Honest."

"It doesn't matter," said the Baba. "Just by seeing us together, Mr. Fisher now knows too much."

"That's right," I said. "Boy, was I surprised when Lt. Sanchez told me about your little Panamanian gang. *Los Osos*, wasn't it?"

"Lt. Sanchez?" the Baba was surprised. Solis was not so easily fooled. "The police know nothing," he said. "Whatever Fisher knows, our friend Pedro told him."

"No, not me. I didn't say nothing." Rawson's fear and nervousness was getting contagious.

"Take them away and dispose of Mr. Fisher." The guy with the pistol took it away from my throat and hit me in the side of the head with it.

"Not here, Octavio," Solis chided. Octavio. What a nice name for a killer. "Take him away." We were dragged out of the limo, with Rawson's protests becoming unintelligible under his blubbering. One of them opened the trunk of the other limo, and threw us both in. Just before they closed the trunk lid, one of them produced an automatic with a silencer at the end of the barrel. He put it to Rawson's forehead and pulled the trigger. The sound of him being knocked back into the trunk was louder than the report of the weapon.

The trunk was closed and I was in complete darkness. I could feel the car drive away. I felt my temple, which hurt more when I touched it. Feeling around the trunk, I could make out the spare tire and a shovel, which gave me some indication of what was going to happen to me. I accidentally touched Rawson, and automatically recoiled. He was dead. Now that I knew where he was, I would try not to touch him again.

The road became bumpy and curvy, and I could feel the engine straining slightly. We were in the mountains. The trunk was not as luxurious as the front. I was not enjoying my first ride in a limousine.

Chapter 21

The ride was long, made longer I'm sure by being in the trunk with a dead body on the way to my own funeral. I took the M-16 clip out of my back pocket to make myself a little less uncomfortable. Nervously, I began playing with the clip, popping out the shells, clinking them together like the captain in The Caine Mutiny. I took three of the shells and placed them in the spaces between the fingers of my left hand. Making a fist, I felt the pointed tips of the rounds. I had seen this done once before by a marine in Vietnam. The fact that he was fighting another jarhead is incidental.

When the car finally stopped, I braced my legs against the back of the trunk, looking for as much power as I could muster. The possibility existed, of course, that they could just as easily set the car on fire or drive it into a lake. I had a feeling, however, that Octavio had other plans for me. He was the one who opened the trunk. He squinted when the comparatively bright trunk light met the mountain darkness. My left arm lurched up as he bent over to grab me. I felt the sharp ends of the bullets sink into his face. He fell back screaming. My hand stung, the bullets dropped and I leapt out of the trunk running as I hit the ground. I could make out a lake a short distance from where the car was parked, and I ran for it. Between the screams, I heard yelling in Spanish. I dove into the water just as I heard the report of a non-silenced nine millimeter. I swam underwater about ten yards, and then, still underwater, turned right ninety degrees and kept working my long unpracticed breast stroke until I felt my lungs would burst. Letting myself float to the surface, I gasped for air. I was amazed at how far I swam. It was that adrenaline thing again.

I was slightly disoriented. My only reference points were the muzzle flashes from the shore firing at where I would have been had I kept swimming in a straight line. The shots echoed in the still mountain night air, punctuated by the groans of poor Octavio who had just been hit with a fistful of M-16 cartridges. I stayed low on the surface, treading water as quietly as possible. Around the previously darkened lake, lights began to come on near the shore. This wasn't South Central Los Angeles, after all, and the sound of small arms fire in the night was enough to stir the lakeside residents and vacationers. It shouldn't be long before a sheriff or ranger appeared, depending on where we were. I swam to a small pier where some boats were moored. I swam until my feet hit the bottom and I crawled out of the water, across the narrow rocky beach, and into the trees.

Even in the summer, the mountains can be cold. I had just

emerged from what had been snow just weeks before. Mud and sand clung to me. My shoes made a sloshing sound when I walked. I circled back to where I had so hastily left the limo. Near the back of the vehicle, the luckless Octavio, now with a record of 0-2 against Bob Fisher (I didn't count the night of the burning Mercedes in my record book), lay silent and motionless. Using the car as a shield, I approached him cautiously. He wasn't moving. I didn't get close enough to determine whether he was dead, unconscious, or in shock.

They had conveniently left the keys in the ignition. I eased my way into the driver's seat, still keeping an eye on the gunman who was busy scaring the fish. In the distance I could see the flashing blue and green lights of a sheriff's four-by-four. I started up the limo, pointed it the other way and floored it. The powerful Cadillac engine snapped my head back and slammed the trunk shut in the same instant. I eventually found the lights and found myself driving an extremely long car much too fast on a much too narrow and curving road. The little road led to a bigger road and at the intersection a sign thanked me for visiting Bass Lake and encouraged me to come back often.

At least now I knew where I was. A right turn would take me to Yosemite. I turned left and headed back down the mountains toward San Joaquin. I noticed I was shivering after a while. I was still soaking wet from my swim in an alpine lake, and the limo's air conditioning was still set on 'cool.' After some fumbling, I found the heater switch and turned it on full blast.

When I stopped shivering my shirt was almost dry. My jeans

would take a lot longer. When I reached the rolling hills at the foot of the Sierras, I pulled off to the side of the road. Slipping out of my wet shoes and socks, I got out of the car and walked to the back door. I opened it. The guy I hit with the M-16 was lying comatose in the back seat. So, I had a dead man in the trunk and another near death in the back seat of what could be interpreted as a stolen limousine. I hope I didn't have to explain this to any passing Highway Patrolman right away.

I looked through the sleeping thug's jacket and found a loaded nine millimeter automatic. They must have had a sale on these. I looked in the refrigerator and found bottles of Perrier and cans of Diet Coke. I washed the blood off my hands with the Perrier. I was only slightly relieved that most of it wasn't mine. I had some minor lacerations from punching Octavio with a fist full of bullets. I drank one Coke quickly and opened another to savor on the rest of the ride.

I took the Coke and the cellular phone to the front seat. I put my wet shoes back on and threw away the mudcaked socks. I called Holly and told her to leave her apartment right away, and go to a motel. Get one with an ocean view, I told her. It took a moment, but then she understood. It was a private joke with us. Anglo developers and businessmen would often attach Spanish names to businesses or subdivisions which had no relation to the actual project. Rio Vista, for example, means 'river view,' but this particular shopping center is nowhere near any river to view. Holly's favorite was the Vista Del Mar Motel, a nice enough motel, which means 'view of the sea.' San Joaquin is about two hundred miles from the nearest Del Mar. She realized the importance and significance of my request and didn't ask any questions.

I parked the limo around the block from the Motel Del Mar and walked around until I found Holly's Honda. I shook her car and the car alarm went off. As a rule, I hate car alarms; it just reminds me that someone has a better car than I do. I appreciated Holly's foresight in getting this one, however, as it served as a convenient doorbell, especially since I didn't know what door. The curtains of one of the windows soon parted slightly, followed soon after by a door. Holly turned off the alarm with the remote control, and ushered me in the room.

The room was pleasant—clean, modern, in-room movies, etc. An innocuous Mar-scape oil painting hung above the queen-size bed.

"Can I go swimming, too?" Chris asked, noticing my wet clothes and shoes.

"Maybe later," his mother told him.

I reached into my shirt and extracted the plastic covered computer disc.

"Apple," she said.

"Right. Do you know where we can get one—an Apple computer, I mean?"

"Sure, Chris has one in his room," Holly informed me. "An older one. Another of Mr. Anderson's bartering deals."

I nodded, familiar with Anderson's business practices, but still amazed that five-year-old Chris had his own computer. At his age I had a Daniel Boone coonskin hat.

"I have to go," I told her. "I'll call you later."

"All right."

"Do you want a gun?" I asked her.

"No, I don't think that will be necessary."

"I'm sorry if I've put you guys in any danger," I said.

"That's all right. This is nothing compared to the neighborhood where I grew up."

I said good-bye again. Chris was disappointed that we weren't going swimming.

From the limo, I called Sanchez and gave him the *Reader's Digest* version of my day. "You personally saw them shoot Rawson?" he asked.

"Yes."

"And you've got the body?"

"Yes."

"And Solis' goon?"

"Yes."

"Bring them to Valley General. I'll meet you there."

"All right. And Sanchez...?"

"What?"

"I'm all right. Thanks for asking." He was worried sick about me, I'm sure.

Chapter 22

When I arrived at the hospital, the welcoming committee greeted me. I popped the trunk so they could remove poor Peter Rawson. Paramedics extracted my unconscious passenger and went to work on him immediately. Sanchez looked at my hand. "You'll be all right." I was relieved by his diagnosis and decided not to get a second opinion from any of the dozens of actual doctors in the building.

"You've got to go downtown and give your statement," he told me.

"Where are you going?"

"We're going to the mountains to pick up Yogi, Boo-Boo and the other bears."

"*Los Osos*," I said.

Sanchez grunted, clearly impressed with my grasp of the Spanish language. "I wanna go," I whined. "Please, please, please," I whined more. "I can give you my statement in the car."

He looked at me. "Pleeze," I whined.

"All right. All right."

In the car with Kaprelian driving, Sanchez brought me up to speed on what I had missed. "A mountain deputy sheriff shot and killed a Hispanic man dressed in a suit who was shooting into Bass Lake. The same deputy also found another man lying unconscious near the lake with a bullet in his cheek. I mean, the whole bullet, cartridge casing and all."

"Octavio," I informed him.

Kaprelian got a big kick out of Octavio's misfortune. "You must have been a terror on the basketball court," he said.

"They found a weapon, recently fired, near him," Sanchez continued.

"That would be the one Octavio shot Rawson with," I said.

"Yeah, we figured that," Sanchez said grumpily.

"What's the matter, Sanchez?" I asked. "Isn't this what you wanted? You know, evidence, witnesses, catching the bad guys?"

"It's turned into an alphabet gang bang," he complained.

Cops have their own little language, which often requires some translation for the uninitiated such as myself. Kaprelian offered an explanation. "Because Rawson was killed in the city, we get to arrest Solis and crew. But because they tried to kill you in Madera County, the Madera County Sheriff is now involved. And because Yogi and Baba are now in Mariposa County, we have to call in their sheriffs. And because they kidnapped you, the Federal Bureau of Investigation has joined the chase. They're sure to have violated some other federal statutes as well. And then, because it is drug related, the Drug Enforcement Administration is coming along. And since Solis is an alien, whose illegal activities have compromised his visa, the Immigration and Naturalization Service will be sending a contingent. Am I forgetting anyone?" Kaprelian asked Sanchez.

"The Alcohol, Tobacco and Firearms people should show up because of the arsenal that's supposed to be up there, and to give us the benefit of their experience in Waco with David Koresh and the Branch Davidians."

"Branch Davidians?" Kaprelian said. "Don't know them, but I know the San Joaquin Davidians." They laughed. Only later did I get the fairly weak play on words based on Armenian names all ending in i-a-n.

"Maybe the Temple have violated their land use permit, so the National Forest Service might be on hand," Sanchez suggested. Sanchez and Kaprelian were enjoying themselves. I wonder if they could do "Who's on First?" Earlier in this century, their ancestors were running through the mountains of Mexico and Armenia, respectively. Sanchez's predecessors were probably riding with Villa and Zapata. Kaprelian's family would have been fleeing the Turkish Pasha, who killed at least a million of his fellow Armenians.

"So basically, what you're saying is we've got the SJPD, the MCSD, the FBI, the DEA, the ATF, another MCSD, and the INS all going after these guys," I observed.

"At least," Kaprelian said.

"So who's in charge?" I asked.

They both laughed. “Technically, the Mariposa Sheriff will be in charge since it is his jurisdiction, but they’ll probably defer to the feds,” Sanchez explained.

“FBI or DEA?” I asked.

“What’s the difference?” Sanchez said.

Overhead, we heard a helicopter. “Oh, yeah, don’t forget the CHP,” Kaprelian remembered, referring to the chopper from the California Highway Patrol.

“You know, if they would have killed you,” Sanchez said to me, “there would be no evidence and we wouldn’t be here now.”

I wasn’t sure how to take that.

Chapter 23

The sun was starting to come up as the caravan of representatives from the various state, local, and federal agencies converged on the gate of the Eternal Truth Temple. The guards, realizing what was the better part of valor, surrendered their weapons quietly. In a few moments, dozens of armed men had surrounded both the residence and the pyramid where the Baba and Yogi lived. It looked like the baseball all-star game. A bunch of different uniforms. Dark windbreakers with DEA, and FBI, and POLICE emblazoned on the backs.

We suddenly heard shots coming from the residence area. It seems some of the faithful chose to defend the Temple, or merely wished to avoid a return to prison. The resistance was soon quashed without any loss of life. That was welcome news as there were a dozen or so children in the compound.

At the sound of the firing, the men and women surrounding the pyramid took defensive cover behind their vehicles and drew their weapons—an assortment of pistols, shotguns, rifles and automatic weapons. A uniformed officer, probably a Mariposa sheriff, produced a bullhorn. Before he could use it, however, a robed believer appeared in the door. His hands were in the air. He walked out slowly. When he wasn't immediately gunned down, he was followed by others. Men and women, variously attired, some wearing pajamas, all with their hands raised. When they reached the circle of police cars, they were forced to lie on the ground, searched and handcuffed.

One of the bound, prostrate faithful said the Baba, Yogi and a few others were left in there and they weren't coming out. "Can anyone identify these Yogi and Baba guys?" an FBI guy asked.

"He can," Sanchez volunteered me.

"O.K., when we go in, you come with us," he said looking at me slightly puzzled, since I wasn't wearing an identifying windbreaker. "DEA or ATF?" he asked.

"PhD," I said.

The FBI leader chose a number of his men, gave the Mariposa sheriff some instructions, and then motioned for us to move out. I tapped Sanchez on the shoulder and indicated that I wanted him to go by pulling on his sleeve. He followed without protest. The group approached the pyramid cautiously, spread out, weapons at the ready. I had left the nine millimeter in the limo. It was uncomfortable in my waistband, not to mention unsafe.

We entered the pyramid and the agents and officers began a systematic room-to-room search. A lot of weapons were found, large quantities of cash, and a paper shredder with the power on and still warm, surrounded by a snow bank of thin paper strips. No sign of anyone, however.

Sanchez and I were merely observers, following the leads of the feds and sheriffs who were now excitedly going through the remains of the Temple's spiritual empire. "I have to take a leak," I told Sanchez and walked into the nearby men's room. As I approached the urinal, I heard the too familiar click of an M 16 safety button. I assumed it was being taken off safety, and regretted not bringing along the nine millimeter, after all, regardless of comfort.

I turned to see Rosario Solis holding an M-16 at the hip, pointing it at me. Even in this non-recommended position, he could hardly miss me at this distance. He said something to me in Spanish, words I have heard before without ever learning an exact translation. His expression and tone were enough to get his meaning. He raised the weapon slightly and seemed to tighten his grip on it as if he was already preparing for the recoil. I blinked when I heard the shot. When I opened my eyes, Solis was leaning against the wall. He looked like he was winking at me. It took a second to realize he wasn't winking. His eye wasn't closed. It was missing.

He began to slide slowly down the wall, the hair on what was left of the back of his head painting a vertical red stripe on the wall tile. Out of the corner of my eye, I saw Sanchez, still in his shooting stance, gun in his right hand, supported by the left, elbows locked, feet apart. Sanchez had shot Solis right in the eye. The exit wound was responsible for the wide swatch of blood above his slumped body. I couldn't help but think that they're probably going to have to redo the grout in those tiles.

Sanchez and I looked at each other, and then at Solis, and then at each other again. We might have kept that up indefinitely, but we heard the sound of a helicopter starting up. He bolted toward the sound. I grabbed Solis' rifle and followed him.

We heard voices behind us, but we seemed to be in the lead when we reached the back door. In the distance, at the tree line, a small helicopter was working up enough power to take off. At the controls, I could make out the turbaned head of the Yogi Ben Barr. The Baba was running across the open space between the pyramid and the helicopter. Sanchez yelled at him to stop. He raised his weapon, just as the Baba turned and fired a short burst from an Uzi.

Sanchez went down hard. The Baba kept running backwards like a football defensive back, still firing the Uzi. I had a strange feeling of *deja vu*. I was standing on a hill in the early morning. My feet and pants were damp. There was the sound of helicopters and automatic weapon fire. A small man, dressed in black, was shooting at me. The butt of an M-16 was pressed against my shoulder. I lined up the black-robed Baba in the sights, aiming for his chest, held my breath, and in a momentary lapse, forgot my basic training. Instead of keeping my eyes open and squeezing the trigger, I jerked back on the trigger with both eyes closed. When I looked again, the Baba was on the ground, writhing in pain. He had lost the Uzi. Uniformed officers had him surrounded and covered while the rest of the posse of sheriffs, FBI, and

DEA, et cetera, surrounded the helicopter, ready to blast the Yogi out of the sky. The CHP helicopter hovering directly over him made that impossible, and the Yogi's chopper hadn't achieved sufficient power to take off anyway. The Yogi, realizing all was lost, met his fate with a traditional spiritual technique, crying and pounding his fists against the copter's controls.

I ran to Sanchez who was moaning and cursing, bilingually. He was on his back. His police windbreaker was shredded from the Uzi burst. "Do you want last rites?" I asked him. In one of the great paradoxes of my military career, I was taught not only to kill, but also to be a chaplain's assistant, where I learned such useful things as how to be an altar boy, how to administer the last rights of the Roman Catholic Church, and to assist in a Jewish bris—the ritual of circumcision.

"Are you out of your goddamn mind?" Sanchez responded. He reached underneath him and pulled out a pine cone. "What the hell is this?" he said and threw it aside. "I hate the mountains."

He rolled over on his side and raised up. I noticed a remarkable lack of blood for a man who was just shot with a machine gun. In fact, there was no blood at all. He sat up and opened his jacket, exposing a now dented, yet effective, kevlar bulletproof vest. "Never leave home without one," Sanchez joked nervously. "We probably had an extra one in the car. You shoulda asked."

"Does this mean you don't want the last rites?"

Sanchez laughed weakly, feeling where a round from the Uzi had hit near his collarbone, only inches from his unprotected neck and head. He seemed pleased to be alive. "I suppose a bris is out of the question?"

"What?"

"Forget it," I said.

Chapter 24

There was a seemingly endless series of depositions and statements. Solis was dead. The Yogi was in custody. The Baba was in custody, albeit at the hospital. I missed his heart and hit him in the right kneecap, and shattered it. I hope they give him a cell on the ground floor, because it is predicted that he will have some difficulty in getting around for the rest of his life. Octavio's already bad complexion was further marred by the scars of being punched with rifle shells. He was indicted for the murders of Peter Rawson, Tom Hammerhill, and Angie Fernandes. All charges against Christy Baker were dropped, of course.

There was national news coverage. The FBI and DEA made it sound like they had orchestrated the whole thing from beginning to end. A generation of lawyers and thousands of court hours would be tied up until the end of the century. A bidding war was expected on the Temple's valuable properties, and the television networks are racing each other for the first Movie of the Week.

Holly took Peter Rawson's computer disc, and on Chris' Apple broke his 'unbreakable' code in about 30 minutes. It was based, she explained, on simple Spanish words whose meanings and usage were slightly altered in Chicano slang. Any local street kid, with some computer skills, could have done the same thing, she said. I let her believe that for now, afraid that if she ever realized how smart she really was she'd leave me behind and go become a millionaire without me.

I declined an invitation to be on Nightline. I had been on before and didn't have the fondest memories of my last taste of notoriety. Sanchez appeared on the show, however, in a new suit and gave what he and I know to be the definitive and most accurate narrative of the events. He even had some nice things to say about me, without once referring to me as "Sherlock Shithead." He was particularly impressed with the fact that I wounded the Baba, effectively disabling him, when I could have easily killed him. Ted Koppel was similarly amazed that I could hit a running man in the kneecap at that range.

I had to smile at that. Not at my marksmanship, but at the fact that I had gone about twenty-seven years without having to kill someone and my streak was still intact.

But the big question, not addressed by the local or national news media, was WHY ME?

The Temple had hired me for two reasons. One, to see if I could actually find the missing disc. The Yogi and Baba suspected that Solis, their long-time friend and drug business partner, had stolen the disc himself and was planning to ease them out of the business. The second reason I was chosen for the job is because I was considered to be the perfect patsy. If someone got killed, my exaggerated reputation would make it easy for me to take the blame. Things got more complicated when Solis thought I was working for Mr. Baker, trying to find out about the connection with Sunnyside Savings and Loan with their drug business. This led to the attack in my apartment. The eventual discovery, that Solis wasn't double crossing the Yogi and Baba, and that Angie Fernandes and Peter Rawson had the disc, led to their deaths. Tommy Hammerhill was killed and Christy Baker drugged because it was first assumed they had the disc.

I always expected organized crime to be a little more organized.

The drug business, apparently, makes a person paranoid and suspicious. The Yogi and Baba suspected their partner Solis, their underlings, Fernandes and Rawson, as well as Tom Hammerhill and Christy Baker. Solis thought I had stumbled on to the Temple/Sunnyside Savings and Loan connection. 'Stumbled' is an apt description of my investigative style, as much of all of this had to be explained to me by Sanchez, Kaprelian and Ted Koppel.

I spent the next week essentially sequestered in my apartment. I lived on delivered pizzas, Kung Pao chicken and Diet Pepsi. I read a long book about the One Hundred Years War and a longer book about the Thirty Years War. I watched the NBA playoffs without caring who won. I never enjoyed them more. When they were finally over, and after reading about one hundred and thirty years of war, I felt excited, motivated. I knew what I wanted to do.

I wanted to go shoot some baskets.

Searching my closet, I found some shorts, a T-shirt, and some well-seasoned tennis shoes. My old basketball was even adequately inflated.

I popped in downstairs. Besides keeping the machine of commerce and trade in operation, Holly had diverted all calls and inquiries for me. The only reference to recent events was a copy of the *National Enquirer* on her desk which revealed the startling fact that Elvis had been seen at the Temple.

"Any messages?"

"The usual," she said. "Religious fanatics and kooks wanting to hire you."

"What did you tell them?"

"I made a little deal with another private investigation company. I told them we couldn't handle all the new business we were getting, so I got them to agree to give us a commission on every case we refer."

"And they went for it?"

"I've already deposited two of their checks," she said proudly. "And speaking of checks." She held out two official looking documents. One was the long promised check from Cooper Page for finding the lost sacred disc. Page was a weasel, but I had lived up to my part of the bargain. The other was a check from another law firm I didn't immediately recognize. But then I remembered

Christy Baker's lawyers from the day Tom Hammerhill was killed. Christy must have told them she had hired me, and this was their way of saying thanks for preventing them from actually having to set foot in criminal court. I looked at both checks. "You know, I could have made this much money if I were still a history professor," I said. "In two years, plus teaching summer school."

I handed them back to Holly. "Get these in the bank before someone changes their mind."

"And there's this." Holly handed me another envelope. It was a Bar Mitzvah card from my brother. When I got married, he sent me a Hannukah card. When I got divorced he sent me a Valentine's Day card. It was an old joke that, to me, grew funnier in the repetition.

As I was about to leave, Christy Baker appeared in the doorway. She was wearing a white T-shirt and a pair of those fashionably torn Levi's.

"Hi," she said. "How are you?"

"I'm all right," I said, holding my basketball.

"I came to say good-bye."

"Goodbye?"

"I'm going away to school."

"Really, where?"

"Bowdoin College."

"In Maine?"

"Yes, do you know it?"

"Yeah, I've spoken there," I said.

"It's about as far from here as I can get." I secretly hoped that here meant her parents and the Temple rather than me.

"Nathaniel Hawthorne went there, you know," she said.

"I know. So did Franklin Pierce."

"Who?"

"Franklin Pierce, our fourteenth president."

"Oh."

"I think you'll like it there," I said. "Just remember, dress warmly."

"I'm going to stop at L.L. Bean on the way." There was an awkward silence as we just looked at each other. "I don't know how to thank you," she said.

"That's all right," I said, wanting to say something else, but I didn't know how. "Just don't get in any trouble up there. I'm not licensed for Maine."

She smiled.

"Call me sometime," I said. "I'll get you a card."

"No, I know your number," she said, and kissed me gently on the cheek.

I watched her leave and stood there for some time before I felt Holly staring at me.

"Well, I'm off. I'm going to shoot some baskets," I said.

"Can I go?" It was little Chris.

He looked at me, smiling, expectantly hopeful. Holly started to admonish him, but I interrupted her. "Sure, why not. Let's go."

He kissed his smiling mother goodbye and we walked to a nearby school.

We played one-on-one to twenty-one points. I spotted him twenty points and still managed to beat him three games out of three. He was a determined player though, and never gave up. The day would no doubt come when he would spot me twenty and still beat me.